## "I had to see you, Laurel."

Nick's voice was thick with passion. "I had to hold you like this."

"Oh, Nick," Laurel breathed. She was playing with fire, she knew. But it felt so good to have his arms around her, so wonderfully right to have his green eyes gazing at her with undisguised desire....

"I'm not going to lie and say I don't want to make love to you," he continued in a whisper. Quickly, playfully he kissed her lips. "But I'll give you time—all of two minutes!"

## THE AUTHOR

JoAnn Ross wrote her first romance in the second grade—with mallards as her hero and heroine. Twenty-nine years later she sold her first full-length novel, and she hasn't looked back since. She's had books published under her own name as well as the pseudonyms JoAnn Robb and JoAnn Robbins.

This bubbly author lives near Phoenix, Arizona, with her husband and teenage son. An incurable optimist and a romantic at heart, JoAnn firmly believes in happy endings.

## Books by JoAnn Ross

**HARLEQUIN TEMPTATION**

42–STORMY COURTSHIP
67–LOVE THY NEIGHBOR

# Love Thy Neighbor

## JoANN ROSS

## Harlequin Books

TORONTO • NEW YORK • LONDON
AMSTERDAM • PARIS • SYDNEY • HAMBURG
STOCKHOLM • ATHENS • TOKYO • MILAN

To Lori Copeland
for always being there when I need her
and for making me laugh.
Here's lookin' at you, kid.

Published July 1985

ISBN 0-373-25167-X

# 1

SHE'D DONE IT! Dr. Laurel Britton, the ex-Mrs. Geoffrey Britton, had successfully moved her household, consisting of one four-year-old Siamese cat, one seven-year-old boy and one thirty-year-old physician all the way from Seattle, Washington to Phoenix, Arizona, without a single mishap. Except for a burst radiator hose, and that could have happened to anyone. Even Geoffrey.

Unfortunately, the unscheduled stop in Indio, California was the reason for Laurel's arrival in a strange town, two days behind her furniture. The long Veterans Day holiday only complicated matters, but after a disgusting display of feminine wheedling, something she personally detested, as well as the promise of holiday overtime, she'd persuaded the moving company to deliver her furniture. Due to start first thing tomorrow as the newest physician at the Phoenix Sports Medicine Clinic, the last thing she needed was all her worldly possessions locked up in a warehouse somewhere across the sprawling desert city. The utility company, regrettably, had proved less helpful and so far no one had shown up to turn on her electricity or her water.

At least the movers were nearly finished. According to her checklist, the only piece of furniture left on the truck was her piano. She watched as the younger of the two men bent to check the canvas strap that held the ancient upright on the dolly.

"Is this an antique?"

Laurel smiled, remembering how long it had taken to refinish the two-hundred-dollar instrument. She and Geoffrey had bought it at a flea market, the expense far too extravagant for two medical students, but she'd fallen in love with it at first sight, and in those days Geoffrey had occasionally found her enthusiasm a delight and not an embarrassment.

"No," she murmured, "it's just very old."

"My gram has one kinda like this. She's got it covered with one of those lacy doily things and tons of pictures of all the relatives."

"I keep pictures on mine, too," she offered, thinking to herself that only photos of Danny remained these days.

"Yeah, I guess everyone does that with pianos all right," he agreed cheerfully, looking back over his shoulder. "Ready, Mike?"

The only response from the man at the other end of the piano was a grunt, which Laurel determined must be a yes since the piano started to make its way down the sloping ramp. She breathed a sigh of relief, drawing a firm, straight line through the listing on her inventory.

Just as she was congratulating herself on having passed her first test in desert survival, an apparition about four feet tall appeared around the corner of the orange-and-black moving van. In place of its face was the huge single eye of a blue swimming mask and a snorkel extended upward from where a mouth should have been. Long black rubber flippers flapped noisily against the sidewalk.

"I'm all ready to go swimming, mom."

Laurel's eyes scanned the immediate vicinity. "Danny, where is Circe? Aren't you supposed to be watching her?"

No sooner had the question escaped her lips than she heard a strident yowl, the high sound peculiar to

Siamese cats. That feline complaint was directly followed by a series of rumbling barks that undoubtedly registered on Richter scales all over the state.

"Danny, catch her!"

Laurel's warning came too late. A flash of creamy fur darted between her legs, followed immediately by one far larger, the color of dark golden caramel. The enormous animal pursuing her fleeing cat plowed into Laurel, knocking her off her feet, and as Circe made a beeline for the open moving van, Laurel opened her mouth to shout out a warning.

From that point, things appeared to happen in slow motion. Sprawled on the blistering hot sidewalk, Laurel watched helplessly as her frightened cat sprang through the air, landing with feline grace on all fours atop the upright piano. The dog was slower, but still swifter than the mover as he rammed into the back of the man's knees. With a colorful series of oaths, the young man fell off the ramp, and to Laurel's fascination her piano rolled down the ramp onto the sidewalk, continuing unrestrained down the hill, headed directly for a jet-black Ferrari parked at the curb. Circe was still riding shotgun, screaming bloody murder at the top of her lungs, her high Siamese yowls shattering the sultry morning air.

"Mom, it's going to hit that car!"

"Of course it's not," Laurel assured her son, jumping to her feet to chase down her runaway piano. "When it hits that speed bump, it'll have to stop."

The young mover was still cursing a blue streak, his epithets competing with Circe's wild howling and the huge furry dog's enthusiastic barking. Laurel had almost caught up with the dolly when it hit the bump in the asphalt, flinging Circe through the air in a long, high arc. The cat landed spread-eagle on the roof of the sports car, her long talons making a screeching sound against the metal top like finger-nails on a chalkboard.

Laurel's prediction proved false as the speed bump only caused the dolly to slow on its inevitable colli-sion with the Ferrari. She was a mere six inches away, her hands outstretched, when the sound of crunching metal blended with the shattering of wood. Laurel stopped in her tracks, staring at the pile of mahogany that was once her beloved piano.

"What in the hell is going on out here? World War III?"

The loud, masculine shout had her spinning around to view a man striding furiously toward her. He was clad simply in a pair of faded cutoffs, worn low on the hips. His sun-streaked blond hair was tousled, and from the blistering expression on his face, Laurel decided he probably wasn't the Wel-come Wagon representative.

"What do you people think you're doing?"

Before Laurel could answer, his green eyes cut to the rumpled fender of the Ferrari.

"Damn."

He raked his fingers through his hair, ruffling it even further as he rolled his eyes toward the blue desert sky. "Wasn't yesterday's game enough? Do you have to add insult to injury?"

Dropping almost gingerly to his knees, he ran his fingertips over the crumpled metal. "Why me? Of all the houses on all the streets in Phoenix, why do I get Laurel and Hardy for neighbors?"

"Laurel and Danny," Laurel corrected with vastly more calm than she was feeling at the moment.

His expression, as he dragged his rueful gaze from his car, was blank. "What?"

"Laurel Britton," she offered, holding out her hand in what she hoped he'd take as a conciliatory gesture. "And my son's name is Danny."

"*You* have a son?"

For the first time since he'd come storming out there, the man's interest turned to Laurel. She was definitely not the teenager he'd taken her for at first glance, Nick McGraw determined. His appraising green gaze moved from the top of her head, tracing every curve and plane, down to her sneaker-clad feet, the journey taking far longer on the way back to her brown eyes. No, this pleasantly disheveled individual was definitely all woman, albeit too slender for his taste. Nick sought an appropriate word and came up with willowy. That fit, he decided, his expert eye taking another slow, leisurely tour of her body.

Laurel had had her share of professional athletes as patients—tennis, baseball, basketball players—all men in peak physical condition, their bodies hard and well toned. But this man, whose gaze seemed to be searing through the thin cotton of her T-shirt, was different. From his challenging stance, to the rock-hard strength of his coppery chest, to the muscled columns of his legs, he was almost too rawly masculine.

She wanted to push back the dark chestnut hair that was clinging in damp strands to her forehead, but withheld the impulse, finding it somehow too feminine a gesture to make before this stranger who was definitely all male.

His gaze slid to Danny, who'd managed to corral Circe and was holding the cat against his chest, his eyes wide blue saucers behind his swim mask.

"So the midget from the Black Lagoon is yours. You don't look that old. What were you, a child bride?" It wasn't meant as a compliment to her youthful looks. The mockery in his voice was unmistakable.

"The *midget* is a seven-year-old boy." Laurel laced

her tone with acid sarcasm. "And I don't see that my age when I married is any of your business."

His answering smile was deliberately provocative, meant to annoy. "Sorry, it's just difficult to believe a grown woman could behave so irresponsibly. I hope for the safety of the neighborhood, your husband keeps you on a tight leash."

Laurel pulled herself up to her full height of five-foot-six. "I beg your pardon?"

"Of course you do," he countered. "And not only do you owe me an apology, don't you think it's time to let me in on what you're going to do about fixing my car?" He looked down at her, his crossed-arm pose exuding arrogance.

As furious as Laurel was becoming, knowing the horrible man was baiting her every step of the way, she also accepted the fact that her piano had careered into his car. Surely her insurance would cover the cost of repairs. She opened her mouth to tell him that when a huge golden ball of fur galloped up, the wide banner of his tail wagging happily, his long red tongue hanging out.

"That animal is yours?" She stared as the man absently patted the beast atop its massive head.

"This *animal* is a registered golden retriever," he corrected. "And yes, Rowdy belongs to me."

Laurel's gaze moved slowly from the dog to the pieces of wood and wire that had once been her beloved piano. Why should she pay anything to fix his car when his beast had caused all the problems in the first place?

"I'd say you're a little confused," she stated finally. "The question here is what are you going to do about my piano?"

One tawny blond brow climbed his forehead before crashing down to join the other. "Lady, you're not only a menace, you're downright certifiable!

Why should I do anything about your piano? After all, my car was parked at the curb, minding it's own business, when your battered old hunk of wood attacked it."

"After your monster attacked Circe!"

"Circe?"

"My cat." She jerked her head in the direction of the Siamese, whose creamy fur was still standing on end, bristling as if caught in an electric storm.

He ran an exploratory finger over the roof of his car. "That explains this bit of vandalism. Claws." His glance flicked rapierlike over Circe. "I don't like cats."

On cue, Circe hissed. "Then you're even," Laurel retorted, with a shake of her dark head, "because she doesn't like you."

She knew her behavior was infinitely childish. They were acting like two kindergartners fighting at opposite sides of the sandbox, and from the bright interest in Danny's eyes, Laurel realized her son was as amazed as she by her atypical behavior.

The glowering man flung his hand over his chest and Laurel attempted not to notice his skin was tanned to the color of teak. Just as she vowed not to be affected by how the blond arrowing of curly body hair disappearing below his belt gleamed gold in the desert sun.

"Come on, lady," he drawled sarcastically. "You're breaking my heart."

"Impossible. You don't have one."

As he returned her glare, the antagonistic mood was suddenly broken by the older of the two forgotten moving men. "Hey, I know you. Nick McGraw, right?"

"Right," her neighbor responded, not moving his gaze from Laurel's face.

"Saw the game yesterday and I can't figure out

why the papers keep clamoring for Morgan. As far as I'm concerned, you *are* the Thunderbirds, Nick!''

To Laurel's amazement, Nick McGraw's face broke into a wide grin and he laughed, a deep hearty sound. ''Now here's a man who knows his football.''

''Gosh, we're sorry about the accident, Nick.'' The younger man joined his partner. ''It just got away from us. But don't worry, our company will make things right.''

Laurel's jaw dropped as Nick waved his hand uncaringly. ''Hey, don't worry about it. Accidents happen. It's no big deal. I shouldn't have been parking on the street, but we had a party last night and I never got around to moving it back into the driveway.''

Laurel furiously decided the truth was he wouldn't have been able to stand, let alone drive.

''I sure hope we didn't wake you up, Nick. We had to get started early because of this heat. Damn, but it's hard to believe it's November!'' The man named Mike wiped his brow with a sweat darkened handkerchief.

Nick turned a rueful glance to the Ferrari, realizing he'd yet to take the window sticker off the new car. However, these days he needed all the fans he could get. There sure wasn't any point in alienating these two.

''That's okay,'' he assured them with a wry grin. ''I had to come out to move my car, anyway.''

The static of a radio in the cab of the van filled the air as the men were instructed to return to the warehouse if finished.

''We'll have our boss call you about the car first thing tomorrow morning,'' Mike assured Nick once again.

''Fine.''

''Well, little lady, if you'll just sign here, we'll be on our way.''

Laurel tried not to visibly bristle at the chauvinistic term. "What about my piano?"

"Don't worry, it's insured. You paid for it when you signed the contract in Seattle."

Since all the king's horses and all the king's men would never be able to put her beloved instrument together again, Laurel neglected mentioning she'd rather have her piano than the money. She sighed as she signed the form.

"Sixty cents a pound." Mike threw the words back over his shoulder as he walked toward the truck.

"What?"

"Sixty cents a pound. That's what the insurance pays off. You'll probably be getting a check in six weeks or so. Enjoy your new house, lady."

"Sixty cents a pound?" She stared after them. "That's ridiculous!" But an answer wasn't forthcoming as the garish van drove off down the curving hillside. She turned on Nick McGraw, her exhaustion, frustration and the blazing Arizona sun making her words rash.

"How come your dog caused all this trouble, but they knock themselves out for you and all I get is sixty cents a pound?"

"Simple. I'm a star."

That much was true. Or at least it had been, Laurel admitted inwardly. Nick McGraw, quarterback for the Phoenix Thunderbirds football team, had been one of the golden men of the game. She'd read about the injury that had sidelined him most of last season and wondered if he was actually going to try to defy the medical experts and return to play another full season.

"I see. So that makes everything you do just wonderful, right?"

"Hey," he objected, "don't forget, I'm the innocent bystander here. After all, you did damage my brand-new car, which in some circles would be considered a hanging offense. Not to mention the fact that you single-handedly shattered the peace and quiet of the neighborhood. It *is* a holiday, you know.''

"I know," Laurel said with heartfelt frustration. "The power company has made that perfectly clear." She eyed the huge adobe house next door, wondering how he'd been able to hear the commotion from indoors. "I was told these homes are virtually soundproof. The realtor assured me they were built that way for energy conservation."

Amazingly, Nick appeared honestly chagrined and shoved his hands into his back pockets. Laurel tried not to notice how the faded denim cutoffs hugged his flat stomach even more tightly.

"Yeah, they are," he surprised her by admitting. "But it doesn't do much good if you're sleeping outside now, does it?"

Laurel's judicious gaze swept over his rugged face, settling momentarily on those disconcerting green eyes. She imagined under normal conditions they'd be devastatingly gorgeous. But this morning the whites were veined with red lines, like a Rand McNally atlas. It must have been one heck of a party next door last night.

"Next time try crawling indoors," she counseled, turning back toward her own house.

"Next time be a little more considerate and I won't have to," he countered. "Besides, crawling is definitely out. Bad knees."

She turned back. This time her gaze was purely professional, dropping down to study the scars crisscrossing his legs. Whatever else he was—rude, unneighborly, arrogant—the man's legs were enough to make her cry.

"I've never seen legs in worse shape."

The resultant light in his eyes seemed oddly impersonal, giving Laurel the feeling the seductive gleam was more automatic than due to any fact he found her more appealing than he had a moment before.

"That's what they all say," he agreed cheerfully. "You've no idea how many woman can't wait to take me home and play nurse."

At the same time Laurel resented Nick McGraw's masculine self-confidence, she didn't believe he was exaggerating. The man was, with the exception of those battered knees, a magnificent physical specimen. His *Playgirl* centerfold had adorned the wall of the women's lounge in her Seattle hospital, and she knew the average woman drooling over that physique had not been looking for scars.

"Nick? Could I have your autograph?" Danny was standing beside them, staring up with undisguised hero worship.

Nick surprised Laurel by remembering her son's name. "Sure, Danny. Are you a Thunderbirds fan?"

"Kinda. But I'm really a Seahawks fan. My dad took me to some of the games. I saw the Thunderbirds play last year in Seattle, but you were out and Morgan was the quarterback. He was pretty good. You guys beat us."

At the dark expression moving across Nick's face, Laurel realized the topic of his replacement was not a popular one, but she couldn't stop Danny's next words.

"Is Morgan taking your place as starting quarterback, Nick? Or is your knee all better?"

"No, to the first. Yes, to the second," he said in a grim tone that made Laurel wonder how much was determination and how much was medical fact.

"Golly, wait until the guys back home hear I live next door to Nick McGraw!"

Danny's young face wore an expression of absolute bliss, making Laurel realize her son had just found something positive about this hard-fought move to Phoenix. While she certainly didn't appreciate the way Nick had come storming over here like an ill-tempered Titan, she had to be thankful for his effect on Danny.

"Why don't you put Circe in the backyard?" she suggested, casting a wary eye at the squirming cat and the bright brown eyes of the dog as he looked ready to begin round two. "Then you can get your football for Mr. McGraw to autograph."

"Neat-o idea, mom," Danny agreed instantly, heading in a trot toward the house. Both adults were silent, watching him leave.

"Mom," Nick murmured, rubbing his jaw. "That's still a bit hard to believe." His gaze cut quickly to her left hand. Laurel was faster, shoving it into her pocket. "Is there a dad?"

She gave him a saccharine smile. "Of course. Didn't your father ever tell you about the birds and the bees?"

"Nope. I learned all that mushy stuff from Mary Jane Marshall in the back of her father's pickup."

"And I'm certain you were a fast learner," she retorted, finding his teasing grin both irritating and boyishly attractive. "So you shouldn't have had to ask that question in the first place."

Nick wondered why it bothered him that Laurel Britton was married. After all, she definitely wasn't his type. She was too slender, her body lacking the voluptuous curves he normally admired in women. Her hair was neither tawny red nor shimmering blond nor gleaming jet. It was simply a nice glossy chestnut, and she'd tugged it back into a ponytail. Her eyes were rather nice, he decided—dark, like those of a gentle doe and sparked with an intelligence he was not used to viewing in his women. *Your women? Knock it off, McGraw, she's taken.*

The unfathomable emotion in Nick's eyes as they settled on Laurel's face made her distinctly uneasy, and she realized belatedly she was holding her breath. *This is ridiculous*, she chided herself mentally. The man was a womanizing jock whose IQ was probably a smaller number than his neck size. What did she care what he thought of her? He was definitely not her type.

"Mom?" Danny's reappearance shattered the oddly unnerving silence.

"What is it?"

"I can't find my football."

"Don't worry, Danny," Nick reassured him. "The Thunderbirds haven't put me on waivers yet. I'll be around at least until you get everything unpacked."

"Thanks, Nick." Danny's expression was beatific. "Mom, can I go swimming like you promised? I'm all ready."

"Not until tomorrow when the man shows up to test the water," she told him apologetically.

She'd used the pool as a bribe to make Danny feel more enthusiastic about leaving his friends, neighborhood and school. And although Laurel felt like the Wicked Witch of the West, she didn't know the first thing about taking care of a swimming pool.

"Ah gee, mom. Nobody ever checks the water in the lake and I've never croaked of nothin' yet."

"Of anything, Danny," she corrected absently, feeling the brilliant green gaze still on her back. "Haven't croaked, er, died of anything yet."

"See?" He pressed on with childish logic. "The lake's filled with all sorts of slimy stuff—tadpoles, fish, water skippers. I didn't see noth-, uh, anything like that in the pool."

"The slimy things in the pool are too small to be

seen by the naked eye, Danny." Nick's deep voice
backed Laurel up. "Want me to show your dad how
to check that pool?"

There was a long, uncomfortable silence and Laurel cried inwardly as Danny's small face fell. *Damn*,
she felt like screaming, *not now! Not when I'm hot and
tired and sticky.*

In her attempt to shelter Danny from the fact that
his father found him less than enjoyable as a full-
time experience, Laurel had brushed over far too
many missed weekends together. She'd thought it
important for her son to believe he had two parents
who loved him equally.

That mistake had come home to her when she'd
been offered this opportunity in Phoenix. They'd
gone through two months of temper tantrums and
when she received a call from Danny's second grade
teacher that the normally easygoing youngster was
behaving no better at school, she'd blithely promised
him he could spend Christmas with his father. And
Geoffrey's *perfect* wife. With that promise, and the
lure of a swimming pool in his own backyard,
Danny had given in.

"My dad lives in Seattle."

So she was a free agent after all. Interesting. Nick's
green eyes moved to Laurel and he nodded thoughtfully.

"Hey, the offer still stands; I'll teach you instead.
This is a pretty big place for your mother to be handling all alone."

He looped his arm around Danny's shoulder and
headed off in the direction of the backyard before
Laurel had a chance to speak. Her irritation rose
even further when she considered Nick's chauvinistic tone. As if she was some hothouse flower who
couldn't function without a male. She'd done just
fine for some time now and could certainly continue

to survive without any assistance from a man who probably only saw women in one role—that of cheerleader.

"I've hired a pool service to do that," she pointed out coolly.

He shrugged wide shoulders. "Hey, don't sweat it. I'll be right back." As she watched, he strode off across the decking to a cedar gate in the six-foot-high adobe wall separating the two backyards.

"I didn't see that gate the first time I was here," she complained, unreasonably disturbed about Nick McGraw's having such easy access to her yard.

"The place belonged to a friend of mine. We built the gate to make things easier."

"I'll bet," she muttered, picturing romantic nocturnal visits.

"J.D. was a running back for the Thunderbirds. He had to sell the house when he was traded to San Diego," Nick enlightened Laurel, his dancing eyes letting her know he'd read her thoughts.

"J.D. Neeman? I'm living in J.D. Neeman's house?" Danny's eyes widened behind the ridiculous mask he'd been wearing almost the entire drive down from Washington.

"Yep," Nick called back over his shoulder.

"Wow, mom. Think of that." He stared around the backyard, whispering as if in a shrine.

"Think of that," she echoed, not having the faintest idea who the man was, but happy that the idea of living in his house gave Danny inordinate pleasure.

Taking advantage of Nick's absence, Laurel escaped to the bathroom, trying to brush her shoulder-length hair into some semblance of order. The adolescent ponytail, while effectively getting her hair off the back of her neck, was less than appealing.

"Look at you," she criticized her reflection. "You're

grimy, sweaty and those clothes should've been put in the rag bin months ago."

It was amazingly hot inside the house and she reached into the shower, twisting the knob as if perhaps the fates would smile on her and make water magically come out, despite the fact the man from the water company had yet to make an appearance.

"I've got water over at my place."

Laurel glanced back over her shoulder to view Nick leaning laconically against the doorframe to her bathroom. "Look, McGraw," she said tiredly, "I don't know what type of open-door relationship you had with your running back friend, but consider things changed." She belatedly regretted her snippy tone, but not the words so she remained silent as his eyes darkened dangerously.

He lifted his hands in a gesture of self-defense. "Hey, lady, don't get so uptight, okay? Your son sent me to find you so you could learn how to test the chemicals, too. He says you're good at stuff like that." His voice held a question.

"If I can light a furnace without burning down the house, I suppose I can learn to detect algae in a swimming pool," she agreed, meeting his gaze with a challenging one of her own. "After all, how hard can it be? If a *football player* can do it?"

Nick crossed his arms over his bare chest, barring her way as effectively as if a mountain had suddenly sprung up in her doorway.

"I think this is where I let you know I'm not wild about dumb jock remarks."

"Then we're even. Because I'm not ecstatic about dumb, helpless women remarks, either."

The silence swirled about them in the stifling heat of the room. Finally, he rubbed his jaw thoughtfully. "I suppose, if we're going to be neighbors, we ought to forge some type of truce."

"Or we can just stay in our own yards," she suggested pointedly.

He ignored her words, wondering what it was about this woman that both annoyed and intrigued him all at the same time. "It's going to be hard for this old dog to learn a new trick, but I'll try if you will." His green eyes encouraged complaisance, while his lopsided grin was expertly disarming.

"For the sake of peace," she agreed, brushing her damp hair off her forehead. "Now, will you let me out of this blast-furnace before I faint '

"I thought I was supposed to think of you as a woman incapable of swooning."

Laurel knew he was laughing at her. "Move, McGraw, or I'll test out that new knee with the toe of my sneaker."

He let her by. "That wasn't funny, Laurel," he murmured in her ear as she moved passed him.

"Neither are you, McGraw. Neither are you."

The unseasonably hot November sun beat down on her head as Laurel dangled her bare feet in the cool water, knowing if Danny wasn't here she'd slide into the inviting turquoise depths, not worrying about algae and pH and all those other important items in Nick's portable test kit.

"It's okay," he announced, after making both Laurel and Danny do the tests three times in order to make certain they'd learned. Laurel thought about all the advanced chemistry classes she'd taken in medical school and almost laughed as Nick led her through the procedures at an excruciatingly slow speed. "The pH is a little high, but I've got some acid over at my place I can give you."

"Thanks, but I'll get my own."

"You don't believe in neighbors borrowing from one another?"

"Not really. It just makes for complications."

"And you're a lady who doesn't like complications."

She nodded firmly. "Right." It was a warning and they both knew it.

Laurel was surprised at the sudden flash of heat that seared through her as Nick's steady green eyes held hers. She tried to blame her increasing vertigo on the blazing ball of desert sun overhead but knew the source of warmth came from something much nearer. A dangerous man, she warned herself. Despite his display of boyish charm, Laurel knew Nick McGraw was nothing but trouble.

"Hey, mom, Nick! Watch me go off the diving board!"

"It's Mr. McGraw," Laurel corrected automatically, her gaze moving to her son.

"Let him call me Nick. All the kids do."

"I don't believe in children calling adults by their first names," she countered.

"Then we shouldn't have any problem."

"Oh?" Her arched brow invited elaboration.

"Since I've the distinct impression you don't put athletes in the same category as adults. Can he swim?" Nick asked under his breath as Danny walked out onto the short fiberglass board.

"Like a fish. And you're wrong. I happen to like athletes." Professionally, she meant, but realized a moment later Nick was determined to take it the wrong way.

"Terrific. This might turn out to be a friendly neighborhood after all."

The leer was automatic. She knew it was. "You know, you're right," she surprised him by admitting freely.

"I am?"

"You *are* an overgrown adolescent. And if you don't quit drooling over me like I'm your own personal smorgasbord, I'm going to call your mother to take you home.''

"You know something, Laurel?"

"What?"

"You get far too uptight about the little things. I think you need to cool off."

Before she could open her mouth, Nick's hands were on her shoulders, pushing her into the water. As Laurel bobbed to the surface, she bit back the stream of epithets that came to mind, none of them remotely appropriate to shout in front of her son. But she would have had to yell them at Nick's back because he was sauntering toward the gate in the shared wall, closing it with a decisive bang.

# 2

LAUREL PULLED HER CAR into the parking lot of the Phoenix Sports Medicine Clinic forty minutes late her first day on the job. So much for establishing a professional image right off the bat, she groaned inwardly. This was definitely not the recommended A.M.A. method to create a terrific first impression.

"I'm sorry," she apologized, rushing into Dr. Matthew Adams's office in a swirl of crisp linen skirt. "But it took longer to get Danny enrolled in school than I'd expected."

The older man's cool gray eyes observed her steadily. "That's quite all right, Dr. Britton. I understand."

While his words were studiously proper, Laurel recognized her superior's expression. And the tone. She knew that although he'd hired her for her skills, the jury was still out on whether a less-qualified male physician might not prove ultimately more suitable.

"It won't happen again," she assured him, feeling unreasonably like a first-year intern.

He nodded an iron-gray head. "I'm pleased to hear that. We need to know we can count on you to be both prompt and efficient, Dr. Britton." It was definitely an order, and while the commandment might not have come from above, Laurel had no doubt it was written in stone. "Now, Doctor, let's go over your schedule."

She'd toured the clinic two months previously,

finding it exactly what she'd been seeking. The field of sports medicine was fairly new; her specialty had not yet been recognized as a standard residency program and the doctors practicing in the field were basically self-educated after first obtaining their medical degree and licenses. In Laurel's case, much of her ability to treat basic overuse injuries and odd ailments came from painful experience, a result of her own dedication to daily running. Additional knowledge was acquired through extensive reading and working in a clinical practice with otherwise healthy patients.

Despite the lack of attention given the specialty in general, this clinic boasted the latest in equipment and the staff were among the best in their field. Laurel knew she was fortunate to be in such company and wasn't about to let Dr. Adams's less than cordial attitude spoil her first day.

The morning went routinely as she treated a constant stream of minor injuries. Taking a breather between patients, she stepped into the doctors' lounge and poured herself a cup of coffee.

"Whew, is it always this busy?" she asked the other occupant of the room.

Dr. Tony Lee grinned sympathetically, his eyes sparkling behind the amber-tinted lenses of his glasses. "Heck no. We cleverly planned all this for your first day, Dr. Britton. Trial by fire—that's Adams's way."

"I wouldn't be at all surprised," she murmured, adding two lumps of sugar to the thick black liquid masquerading as coffee.

"He's not so bad once you get used to him."

"I hear that's what they say about the Ayatollah, too." Laurel took a tentative sip. Grimacing, she added yet another lump of sugar and a heaping teaspoon of powdered creamer.

"I can see nutrition wasn't your specialty." Laughing dark eyes were focused on her plastic cup.

"Did you make this coffee?"

He grinned. "Guilty as charged."

"Then you're in no position to criticize. This stuff would make mud taste great."

"Are you offering to become chief coffeemaker?" There was a laughing challenge in her colleague's tone.

Laurel considered. "If I do, it'll only be because I don't want to leave my child an orphan. Too much of this stuff has to be hazardous to a person's health. It won't be because I'm the only female doctor on staff. Agreed?"

"Agreed. I know I speak for the rest of the staff when I extend my heartfelt thanks, Doctor. They've never been wild about my coffee, either, but so far no one else has volunteered to take up the task." He grinned happily.

"What about you? You can't tell me you like this coffee?"

"I stick to tea bags," he explained, his black eyes twinkling as he lifted his cup to his lips. "It's safer that way."

Laurel laughed as she was supposed to, sinking down onto the soft leather couch. She kicked off her shoes, allowing her feet a few blissful moments of freedom. Wiggling her toes happily, she sipped her too-sweet coffee, priding herself on making it through an unusually hectic morning.

Forced to treat not only her scheduled patients but the emergency walk-ins as well, she had managed to attend to everyone without falling behind. That came as a relief, since she was aware of Dr. Adams's almost constant observation. Laurel had the odd feeling he was just waiting for her to make a mistake. She was scanning the patient list in her hands when one name jumped off the page.

"N. McGraw," she groaned. "Don't tell me."

"Nick McGraw," Dr. Lee agreed. "He was Ben Phillips's patient, before the old man retired. Since you're inheriting his clinic practice, McGraw comes with the territory."

"I'd assume the Thunderbirds have their own physicians."

"They do. But that injury last year seems to have McGraw spooked. He insists on using his own doctors, rather than trust the team physicians."

Laurel could understand that. She'd seen far too many cases of team physicians looking the other way while trainers shot up athletes with enough xylocaine to numb a bull elephant, so they could continue to play. If Nick's injury had been as bad as she'd heard, he was wise to seek outside medical advice. She did, however, hate to think about the possible fireworks when that quintessential male chauvinist discovered his new doctor was a woman.

Dr. Adams entered the lounge, as if conjured up by the hobgoblins of Laurel's darkening mood. Cold gray eyes raked over the two physicians, his expression definitely disapproving as he took in her stocking-clad feet.

"Dr. Britton, I hate to break up this little tête-à-tête, but you have a patient waiting." At Laurel's unconscious glance downward toward her paper, he stated briskly, "An unscheduled emergency. Another one of those three-day-weekend idiots."

As she reached down slipping on her shoes, Laurel wondered idly if there was anyone Dr. Adams *did* approve of. When she'd come to Phoenix to investigate this position, she'd met with the saturnine administrator only once, and that had been a brief, uneventful interview. She'd much preferred the idea of working with the chief of staff, Dr. Jeremy Parrish. Unfortunately, Dr. Parrish had taken a leave of absence to concentrate on new treatments for torn tendons and until a new chief of staff was appointed, Laurel would be working directly under Dr. Adams, a cold fish if she'd ever met one.

"I'll see the patient right away," she said quickly, rising to her feet, more than willing to escape the steady unblinking stare of her superior.

Matthew Adams won the last word. "That was the idea, Doctor."

A young woman was seated on the examining table, her tanned face displaying far more frustration than pain.

"Hi," she greeted Laurel glumly. "I sure hope you've got better news than my family doctor."

"Hi. Let's see what we've got here." Laurel skimmed the chart. "You jog?"

"I run," the woman corrected firmly. "Jogging is for faddists."

Laurel smiled, understanding completely. "I know. I run, too."

The woman's expression perked up and she appeared more hopeful. "You do? Then you'll understand why I can't stay off my foot for two months. I'll go stark raving bonkers!"

Laurel nodded, her fingers probing delicately at the woman's ankle. "How long ago did you get this sprain?"

The woman flinched as Laurel's fingers hit a sore spot. "A few months ago. Five or six," she added sullenly.

"And you didn't slow down your activities, right?"

"I was in training."

Laurel sighed. "I wish I had a nickel for every time

I've heard that. I could have retired in luxury long ago.''

"You're as bad as my family doctor. He says I've got to stay off it entirely," she complained.

Before Laurel could comment, a flurry of activity at the doorway caught her attention. Her patient's interested gaze followed hers to the tall man standing in a circle of ardent admirers.

"Oh, my God, is that who I think it is?" The young woman was practically swooning.

"It is if you think it's Nick McGraw," Laurel replied briskly, determined to ignore that odd twinge deep inside her that his appearance had triggered. "Now, about this ankle..."

"I can't believe it. Nick McGraw! Right here in person." She patted her hair into place and sat up a little straighter.

"In living color," Laurel agreed dryly. "Now, what you've done, Ms Dalton, is exacerbate your injury by excessive movement. You never allowed your sprain to heal in the first place. You should have—"

"He's coming over here," her patient hissed, obviously not hearing a word of Laurel's professional diagnosis.

*Here we go,* Laurel thought to herself, unconsciously holding her breath as she awaited Nick's reaction. She steeled herself for a display of wounded male pride.

As Nick moved toward Ben Phillips's old examining table, he thought the nurse-practitioner seated on the low stool looked oddly familiar. There was something about the slender line of her shoulder and the sleek curve to her chestnut hair. Laurel, he decided, she reminded him of Laurel. But that was ridiculous; he only made the connection because he'd been thinking about his new neighbor far too much during the past twenty-four hours. That prickly female had gotten under his skin and he was damned if he could figure out why.

"Excuse me, but I was told the doctor would see me next."

Laurel turned slowly, keeping her smile brightly professional. "I'll be with you as soon as I finish with this patient, Mr. McGraw."

Nick knew he was staring and struggled to keep his expression nonchalant. Images of his arrogantly male behavior with the pool-testing kit flew into his mind and he wondered if he was actually blushing. He must have looked like a first-class idiot teaching this woman how to read chlorine residuals.

"So it's *Dr.* Britton. This *is* a surprise."

"Isn't it?" she agreed hesitantly, her smile wobbling just a little. Was that dark red flush rising from his collar because he was angry? Laurel desperately hoped not.

She breathed a sigh of relief as he appeared disinclined to argue the point. "Go ahead, Doc." He nodded his blond head toward the young woman. "I'll just sit here quietly and watch you do your medical thing."

"If you'd prefer, you could wait out in the lobby," she suggested hopefully. "There are some magazines there. They're probably ancient, but..." Laurel knew she was rambling, but Nick's steady green gaze was definitely unnerving.

"I've read them all, Laurel," he stated smoothly. "Now, don't mind me. I promise to be so unobtrusive you won't even know I'm here."

Ha, Laurel considered grimly, feeling his gaze riveted on her as she turned back to Jenny Dalton, fat chance of that. She was all too aware of his presence, just as she hadn't missed the way he'd lingered a shade too long over her first name, caressing it in an oddly personal manner. Even her patient appeared to notice, her curious gaze flicking back and forth between Nick and Laurel.

Laurel forced her attention back to the woman's ankle. "You have to understand that doctors who aren't involved in sports themselves have a tendency to be ultracautious. The truth is most injuries will heal faster with sensible self-doctoring and moderate activity."

She pulled the woman's sport sock back up. "Next time you have an injury, treat yourself immediately with ice. Ice, compression and elevation. Then, as soon as possible, gently move the injured part to flush out the fluids and cell debris in the injured area. That'll also help restore normal range of movement."

"Okay," the woman replied in a miffed tone. "So that's what I should've done. Are you telling me it's too late? That I've got to stay off my ankle entirely?"

"Of course not," Laure corrected briskly. "But you must utilize some common sense. How far do you usually run a day?"

"Ten miles."

Laurel chewed thoughtfully on the end of her pen, then began writing on a prescription pad. "Okay, here's what I'm going to suggest. I want you to begin with a three-mile walking and jogging workout. First walk briskly until you're no longer limping, then jog as long as you can without feeling the pain. When the pain starts again, walk until it disappears, then start in running again."

She tapped a stern warning on the pad with her ballpoint pen. "Now remember, the key is to build up cautiously. Try taping the ankle and see if that gives you additional support. And whatever you do, don't increase the stress load until the sprain is healed. Is that clear?"

The young woman nodded, her sulky expression replaced by a wide smile. "Sure, I can handle that. Thanks a lot, Dr. Britton, you've made my day."

"Make mine and allow time for that ankle to heal properly," Laurel cautioned with an answering smile.

"You've got it," the woman agreed, her attention returning to Nick McGraw. "Would you sign an autograph for my kids? They'd kill me if they knew I'd shared an examination table with you and didn't ask."

Nick's attention had been on Laurel. He'd been entranced by her full pink lips and strong white teeth as she'd chewed thoughtfully on that pen. He was going to have to taste those ridiculously sexy lips, he decided. Realizing belatedly that Laurel's patient had spoken to him, Nick forced his mind to her words.

"Kids?" he answered automatically, knowing exactly what the young woman wanted to hear. "You don't look old enough to have kids."

Laurel decided it must be a pat line with the man. Watching the woman's beaming response, she also realized it brought results.

"I've got two.... But, of course I got married right out of high school."

"You sure don't look any older than that now. Running obviously agrees with you."

Nick's expression was masculinely appreciative while unthreatening, and Laurel considered how easily these lines came to him. With those gorgeous green eyes and devastating smile, Nick McGraw must have women falling at his feet.

Taking the piece of paper the woman extended, he glanced over at Laurel, patting the pocketless chest of his polo shirt. "Ah, may I borrow your pen, Doctor?"

Laurel handed it over, jerking back from the odd

shock as their fingers touched. Nick felt it, too; she knew from the bright light suddenly gleaming in his eyes.

"Static electricity," she murmured.

"Of course," he agreed instantly, returning his attention to Laurel's patient. "What are their names?"

Jenny Dalton had been staring, her eyes drinking in so much man only a few feet away. "Names?" she inquired blankly.

"Your kids," he reminded her.

"Oh! Ryan and Megan."

"Nice Irish names," he remarked. "Do they like football?"

"They *love* the Thunderbirds. And of course they think you're the best quarterback in the league."

"It's nice to know I've got a few fans left out there," he said, his words tinged with heavy irony.

"Oh, at least three. I think you're absolutely wonderful, too."

Laurel watched Nick's dispassionate answering smile, noting it didn't extend to his eyes, the way it had when the moving men had complimented his playing ability.

"Thanks." He handed the paper to the woman and the pen back to Laurel.

"Oh, thank you, Nick," Jenny Dalton breathed, eyeing the bold black script. Then her attention returned to Laurel. "Thank you, too, Dr. Britton." She grinned up at Nick. "You're real lucky. She's a great doctor."

"I've always been lucky," he murmured thoughtfully as Jenny floated away, still on cloud nine.

But Nick failed to watch her leave; his attention was drawn to Laurel's face. Her eyes were as wide and as velvety brown as he remembered, her lashes a thick, lush fringe. But why hadn't he noticed those high, delicate cheekbones yesterday? And her lips.

No doctor had any business with lips like that. Lushly pink, and sensually full, they brought to mind physical images that were definitely not of a medical nature. Her rainwater-straight hair was the color of chestnuts, falling in a sleek curve to her shoulders, and he wondered why he'd ever thought redheads more interesting, blondes sexier.

In her own oddly jarring way, Laurel Britton was far more interesting and ultimately sexier than any women of his past experience. His gaze moved over her white lab coat, as he remembered how firm her breasts had been under the damp cotton T-shirt.

"You'll have to take your pants off."

Considering the erotic train of his thoughts, Laurel's words brought Nick up sharply. "What?"

She nodded a glossy head toward his jeans. "Your pants. I can't examine your knee when you're dressed."

For the first time since adolescence, Nick worried about the control he had over his body. Laurel Britton might be a doctor, and from the way she handled that patient earlier, he knew she was probably a damn good one. But she was also a woman. And that was the problem.

"How come I don't rate a private room?" he asked.

Laurel's gaze swept the large room. "They're all being used at the moment."

He crossed his arms over his chest. "Ben Phillips always examined me in a private room."

"Perhaps you never showed up on a Tuesday after a three-day weekend," she countered. "Come on, McGraw, let's see a little cooperation here."

"I'm not used to taking off my clothes in front of strange women."

Laurel's judicious gaze moved over him, taking in his wide shoulders, broad chest and trim waist. Although he was reaching the end of his playing days, Nick's body was definitely not that of a man past his prime. He was in excellent shape, she noticed as a physician. The woman in her admitted he was also gorgeous.

She couldn't help smiling. "Oh, I think you're being overly modest, McGraw. I've the impression you've been known to do exactly that more times than either of us would care to count. Besides, any man who's willing to pose in the nude for *Playgirl* can't be all that shy.... Now, do you take them off, or shall I?"

A thundercloud moved ominously across his dark face. "I wasn't nude."

She waved a dismissing hand. "Well, you certainly couldn't have told that from the photos. The pants?" she reminded him pointedly.

He glanced around the busy examining room. "Not until you put up a screen."

"Oh, for Pete's sake." Laurel expelled a sigh of exasperation, marching across the floor to retrieve the folding screen. She wondered how this man had survived all the years of public locker rooms if he was so blasted shy.

"There.... Now will you cooperate?" She stuck the screen in front of her table, arranging the three sides to supply privacy, remaining outside to allow him to strip down to his underwear.

"Ready."

He was seated on the end of the table, his long legs dangling over the end, and once again she breathed in sharply as she viewed the crisscross scars violating the dark skin covering his knees. While Laurel had seen injuries just as critical, none had ever caused that odd stab of pain somewhere deep inside her.

"That bad?"

"They're not pretty." She shook her head. "Is it worth it?"

"What?"

She nodded in the direction of his legs. "The surgery, the pain, all that. Is it really worth it? Just so you can play one more season?"

"I could ask you how you feel about breathing," he answered simply. "And by the way, it wasn't my idea to pose for that layout. I fought it like hell for months."

Laurel had the odd impression that it was important to Nick that she know that. Why should he care what she thought? She shrugged.

"It really isn't any of my business; it was unprofessional of me to bring it up. I'm sorry."

He refused to let the issue drop. For some reason, he hated that look of disapproval that came into her eyes from time to time. Although he knew it would allow her unwelcome insight into his problems, he wanted to make her understand the desperation that had led to his behavior of the past year. The magazine layout, the parties, his admittedly wild lifestyle. But it was all so complicated. And he wasn't certain he understood himself.

Laurel's fingers pressed against his leg with gentle strength as she examined the injured knee. Nick reached out, cupping her chin in his fingers, lifting her gaze to his.

"My agent insisted that if I was going to be out of action for an entire season, we needed to keep my name out there in front of the public. At least it was better than all the portraits the sportswriters were painting of a washed-up, battered old wreck."

A little voice in the far reaches of Laurel's mind reminded her that this was hardly professional behavior. Her hands were trembling on the man's naked leg, as she drowned in the warm green pools of his eyes. His fingers were literally burning her skin, but she was in no hurry for him to take them away.

She made a weak attempt at levity. "That was not the body of a battered old wreck."

His gaze didn't move from hers. "Then you've seen it?"

"Hasn't everyone?"

"So my agent says," he muttered with self-deprecating humor. "Did you like it?"

"It'll do, McGraw, it'll do."

The smile lit up her face, making her extraordinarily attractive. Nick had a sudden urge to kiss her, and wondered what would happen to the briskly professional Dr. Britton if he pulled the lovely Laurel into his arms and covered those ridiculously sensuous lips with his own.

Laurel felt trapped as she stared into Nick's darkening eyes and every feminine instinct she possessed told her Nick McGraw was about to kiss her.

"Don't," she said softly.

His thumb played at the corner of her lips. "Why not?"

"I'm your doctor." Laurel was grateful she was sitting down as his tantalizing touch turned her bones to melted wax.

"You're also a beautiful woman."

She faltered for a moment, caught up in Nick's desirous gaze. Then her sense of humor saved her and she managed an honest grin.

"Thanks, McGraw. I think I'll take that as a compliment, without worrying about how many times you've already handed it out today."

"Laurel." His voice was husky, rough and soft at the same time, reminding Laurel of ebony velvet.

She shook her head. "Don't complicate things, Nick."

God, what he'd give for just one taste of those luscious ripe lips. "I believe it's a little late for that advice. You must realize I want you, lovely Laurel...."

Laurel's mouth went suddenly dry. "You may want me as a woman, but you *need* me as your doctor," she managed to say after a long silence.

Okay, Nick decided, they'd play the game her way. For now. He'd always enjoyed a challenge and something told him Laurel Britton was going to prove exactly that. But he was going to have her, of that Nick had not the slightest doubt.

He released his light hold on her chin, splaying his fingers on his dark thighs, the gesture intentionally provocative.

"Well then, as my doctor, what's your diagnosis?"

Laurel was shaken, but determined not to show it. "I've seen horses shot for less."

"I'm only planning to play a football game, Dr. Britton. Not run the Kentucky Derby."

She sighed. "Your records show you had your surgery less than a year ago, and unfortunately, tendon tears are the worst injuries an athlete can sustain. I know Dr. Phillips told you to give it at least a year—even eighteen months wouldn't be an unreasonable period of recovery time. Try a little patience," she counseled in her most professional tone.

"I don't have a year." At Laurel's dubious expression, Nick exhaled a frustrated breath. "Look, Laurel—" He hesitated. "May I call you Laurel? I feel a little funny calling you Dr. Britton after yesterday."

"Are you saying you don't normally push your physicians into the pool?"

"No."

"That's a relief." Laurel started making notations on his chart.

"But of course they usually don't ask for it, either."

Her pen stopped in midsentence as she glanced up at him. Nick's expression was bland, but his green eyes were smiling. She allowed herself a slight grin.

"You may have a point. I was tired, out of sorts and aggravated with the world in general. And you didn't exactly welcome me to the neighborhood."

"Hey, whose piano crashed into whose brand-new car?"

Laurel held her ground. "And whose dog attacked whose cat?"

Their eyes locked and finally Nick shrugged. "This argument sounds vaguely familiar."

She wondered what it was about Nick McGraw that had her veering from unwilling interest to infuriating aggravation, all in a span of a few seconds. The one thing he'd yet to do was bore her.

"You're right. Let's drop it. Why don't you spend a half hour or so in the whirlpool?" She nodded her head in the direction of the therapy room. "I'd like to put you on the Cybex and measure the strength of that leg, but there's a line for it a mile long, so I suppose we can save it until next time."

He slid off the table with an exaggerated groan. "I knew it—you're going to abuse my body for your own amusement. You women are all alike."

"If there's any abusing of your body going on, it's going to be in a strictly medical capacity, McGraw." Her words held a definite warning.

He studied her for one full minute, his fingers rubbing thoughtfully at his chin. The longer he was around this paradox of woman-doctor, the more she intrigued him. He found himself wanting to know everything about her.

"Is that a fact?"

Laurel nodded, holding his appraising gaze with a

level one of her own. Even as she allowed herself a fleeting fantasy of how his hard male body would feel against hers, she forced herself to remember their positions.

"Fact."

His eyes held a faint light of amusement as they lingered on her face. "Are you so sure about that?"

Pretending disinterest, she turned away to remove the screen. "Positive."

Nick hated to lose the privacy the temporary wall allowed. He reached out to grasp her arm but common sense overruled more primitive urges. He withdrew his hand and forced a careless shrug.

"Hey, it's okay by me. I just didn't want you kicking yourself when you realized what you'd turned down."

Laurel eyed him curiously over her shoulder. Once again his masculine gaze was unnervingly impersonal.

"I'll survive," she muttered. "You know where the therapy room is; I'll catch up with you as soon as I call Danny's school."

"Is something wrong?" This time the interest in Nick's green eyes was genuine, she realized. As was his obvious concern.

"Not wrong. I'm going to be late picking him up. It's a private school and while it costs a bit more to have them keep him after class, it's worth it for my peace of mind. I don't like the idea of a child as young as Danny home by himself all afternoon."

"But he shouldn't have to stay *there* all day, either," he argued. "When I was Danny's age, I couldn't wait to get out of school."

"I take it your mother didn't work."

"Sure, she worked. At home. Taking care of us kids, cooking, you know—old-fashioned mom stuff."

Laurel detected a hint of sarcasm in his tone and crossed her arms militantly across her white lab jacket. What business did this man have criticizing her parenting? She'd been doing it alone for some time now and while she knew there was always room for improvement, she'd done her best to be both mother and father to Danny, as well as bread-winner for her family.

"I'm not wild about the setup, either, but right now it's the best I've found. So why don't you just mind your own business and spare me the assorted tales from 'Father Knows Best'?"

Nick was surprised by Laurel's unexpected vulnerability. She wasn't as tough as he'd thought. His expression immediately softened.

"You're right. It's none of my business. Although I'd venture a guess this isn't exactly an easy day for you—a new house, a new job, Danny in a new school. It's a lot for one lady to handle."

Laurel's answering laugh was tinged with faint bitterness. "It's a lot for one person—man or wom-an—to handle. But I haven't had a lot of volunteers lately." She began folding away the screen, but this time Nick gave into instinct, reaching out to forestall her progress.

"I'm volunteering, Laurel," he said simply.

She stared up at him, searching his face for the chauvinistic punch line she knew would be coming. "Volunteering? For what?" As soon as the question escaped her lips, Laurel cringed, knowing she'd handed him a perfect straight line. But Nick surprised her by not picking up on it.

"I've got a practice this afternoon after I leave here. Why don't I pick Danny up at school and take him out to the field with me?"

"You've got to be kidding!"

"Not at all. Don't you think he'd like it?"

"He'd love it and you know it. But I couldn't impose like that."

"Complications," he murmured softly, reminding her of their conversation by the pool. "You don't get involved with your neighbors."

Laurel simply nodded, not willing to trust her voice. She couldn't believe he was actually offering to help out of simple kindness. There had to be a catch, yet she certainly couldn't find proof of it in his expression.

"Would you agree if I assured you it would be a big help to me personally?"

"How?" she inquired suspiciously.

"I could use a little moral support today. Although Danny's a Seahawks fan, I'm betting he'll extend a little loyalty to a neighbor."

"It's that rough?" she asked softly. Laurel was honestly surprised to find this strong, rawly masculine man needing moral support from anyone.

"I could ask you the same question," he countered, his tone low enough to keep their conversation from being overheard by anyone else in the room. He expelled a harsh sigh. "Look, this is a year of changes for both of us, so let's just see what happens if we try being friends. I'd say you could probably use one about now and I know I'd feel better knowing someone was in my corner."

Nick knew Laurel was thrown by his suggestion. She dragged her eyes away from his.

"I'm not sure that's a good idea," she decided finally.

"Afraid?" he asked lazily.

The laughing tone in his voice only served to irritate her. "Of course not."

By the way her fingers trembled as she replaced the ballpoint pen in the breast pocket of her starched white lab jacket, Nick knew Laurel was growing angry at his persistence. But she was also affected more than she cared to admit. He pressed his advantage.

"If you're not afraid, what else could you have against a simple neighborly friendship?"

Laurel felt herself being maneuvered, even as she forced herself to study this situation with a somewhat detached eye. Every feminine instinct she possessed assured her there would be nothing simple about any relationship with Nick McGraw. An intimate relationship with the man would be bound to be short-lived, fiery and totally against her own best interests. However, there *was* an outside chance they could maintain some sort of casual friendship.

The mother in Laurel pointed out Nick could certainly help Danny overcome his resentment about leaving Seattle. What little boy wouldn't be in seventh heaven if allowed to spend time with a professional quarterback of Nick's fame and status?

She nodded slowly and they both knew a silent understanding had been achieved. "You've got yourself a deal," she agreed, holding out her hand. "And a weary mother's heartfelt thanks."

As Laurel's slim palm disappeared into his grip, Nick granted himself the pleasure of holding her hand longer than necessary for a casual handshake. Knowing it to be a risky gesture at this point, he couldn't resist lifting her wrist to his nose.

"Mmm, nice. Arpège? Chanel?"

Laurel tugged her hand free, deciding this had to be the shortest truce on record. "Phisohex. And we're talking just friends here, McGraw. So don't forget."

He grinned, a devastingly attractive smile. "Just friends," he agreed cheerfully. Then, giving her a snappy salute, he turned in the direction of the therapy room, apparently oblivious of his underclad state. "Oh, and Laurel?"

On her way to phone the school about her change in plans, she stopped, eyeing him over her shoulder. As he stood so unself-consciously in the center of the room, Laurel realized he'd only insisted on the screen to ensure a chance to speak with her privately. The man was definitely an expert in manipulation. She'd have to stay on her toes.

"Yes?"

Nick waggled his tawny blond eyebrows in an outrageously lustful manner. "I'll pick up something for dinner and when you come home, you're invited to be as friendly as you like."

He winked and was gone before she could destroy him with a few well-chosen words. The resultant roar of laughter from the examining room full of spectators demonstrated that everyone had enjoyed Nick's performance immensely. Everyone, that is, except Dr. Adams, who was eyeing Laurel with overtly cold disapproval.

Forcing herself to ignore the lingering chuckles, Laurel went to dial the telephone number of the school, receiving a maddening busy signal her first two tries. It had already been an incredibly long day and she had the uncomfortable feeling that with Nick determined to call the shots, the evening was bound to prove even more of a challenge.

# 3

LAUREL WORKED WITHOUT a break the rest of the afternoon, the unscheduled patients outnumbering the ones with appointments nearly two to one.

"I hate three-day weekends," she muttered, preparing an immobilizing cast for a teenager who'd pulled a ligament in his knee during a strenuous tennis match the previous day.

"They're the worst," Tony Lee agreed as he studied a set of X rays. "Tell me what you think of this."

Laurel glanced up at the backlit board. "A stress fracture," she diagnosed easily. "But why did you bother with an X ray? The treatment's the same as a bad sprain."

"It's her third this year."

Laurel stopped her work, stripping off her gloves. She moved across the room to stand beside him. "Is she a runner?"

"Long distance."

"Premenopausal amenorrheic?"

"She's thirty-two and hasn't had a normal menstrual cycle for three years," he answered, examining the X ray intently. "I'm thinking about scheduling a CT."

Laurel gave the idea brief consideration, hating to argue with a colleague her first day on the job. The computerized axial tomography scanner detected bone density and she was well aware of the recent findings that indicated women who were hard-training, long-distance runners might be inadvertently causing irreversible damage to their bones. As a runner herself, she'd studied all the data available thus far.

"Why don't you first check her calcium absorption?" she suggested carefully.

"If the woman is suffering from osteoporosis, due to athletic amenorrhea, Dr. Lee's suggested course of action is sound enough." Dr. Adams's voice entered the conversation as he came up behind the pair.

Laurel reminded herself that it would certainly not help anything to get fired by entering into a heated argument with her superior. Giving her words serious consideration, she answered slowly.

"From what I've read on the subject so far, the reports are interesting, but little more than a scare. There's no real factual data. They've lumped a few women runners with fertility problems together with women who have amenorrhea from totally different causes. It's as if we took a test group of individuals who all had broken legs and assumed they'd gotten them in the same way."

Matthew Adams's expression was inscrutable. "Are you saying Dr. Lee should simply ignore the problem?"

She felt Tony's encouraging dark eyes on her, realizing he'd never intended this to end up an inquisition. Drawing a deep breath, Laurel said a silent prayer that she wouldn't offend the younger doctor.

"Of course not. But I still suggest Dr. Lee first check his patient's calcium intake. Then instead of the CT, if he still feels a need to measure bone density, I'd recommend gaining access to a photon absorptiometer instead. Not only does it provide a more precise and accurate measurement, it's less expensive. Plus there's the matter of a much lower radiation exposure."

"The amount of radiation exposure required by

the CT scanner isn't all that significant, Dr. Britton," Dr. Adams pointed out.

Laurel managed a slight smile, mustering up the courage to stick to her point. "That's true, of course. But it's still more than it needs to be. Less would be an advantage because Dr. Lee could test more frequently. With the photon absorptiometer, the patient would only be subjected to what she'd get from the normal background in two weeks. From the CT she'd receive the equivalent of a year and a half's natural radiation."

Laurel decided to jump in all the way. Her words came out in a slight rush. "I know Dr. Parrish applied for funds to purchase the machine. I'd like to second that motion."

Dr. Adams's gray eyes flicked over her face. "Are you always so opinionated, Dr. Britton?"

Laurel's cheeks grew warm at his icy insinuation. "I'm afraid so," she answered honestly. "But only when I have strong feelings about something. As well as the knowledge to back those feelings up."

"Yet you're willing to ignore the fact women runners are possibly in grave danger of risking permanent bone loss."

"I'm ignoring nothing," Laurel argued, her temper starting to flare at his demeaning tone. "I simply believe the findings are preliminary and have been blown all out of proportion by male sports journalists who want to force women off the athletic field and back into the kitchen."

He gave her a sharp glance. "I don't believe this is the place for women's liberation speeches, Doctor. But even if it were, you're a damn poor choice to talk women's equality."

Now Laurel was incensed. She rose up to her full height, forgetting her vow to discuss this issue calmly. "Exactly what do you mean by that?"

"I was referring to your display with that football player." He heaped an extra helping of scorn on the term, his prejudices blatantly obvious. "One day on the job and you're already arranging intimate little evenings at home with one of your patients."

Dr. Adams's eyes were steely little marbles. "Is that why you turned to *sports medicine* in the first place, Dr. Britton?" His tone, when stressing her specialty, was as acid as it had been earlier when stating Nick's.

"That question does not justify an answer."

"It was a rhetorical one, Doctor. After all, it's obvious you'll meet more eligible men in this field than you would in the more traditional women's roles of pediatrician or obstetrician." With that last verbal slap in the face, Dr. Adams turned on his heel and left the room.

"I can't believe that man," Laurel spluttered furiously.

"Neither can I," Tony seconded in amazement. "The man's never been Mr. Personality, but other than asking me the first week I was here why I hadn't gone into acupuncture, he's left me pretty much alone."

"He was probably afraid you'd poison the coffee and he'd never be able to tell until it was too late," Laurel shot back.

Tony laughed appreciatively. "You've got a point." Then his look changed to one of obvious interest. "Uh, I was going to try to figure out how to lead into this gracefully, but since our *führer* already brought the subject up, what's between you and Nick Mc-Graw? This morning you were moaning about meeting the guy."

"I was moaning about *treating* him," Laurel corrected. "I met the man yesterday. Under less than optimum conditions."

"Anything juicy for the clinic's gossip line?"

"Not unless you're into stories from Ripley's Believe It or Not. My piano put a dent in his brand-new Ferrari."

"How in the world did that happen?"

Laurel grimaced. "Believe me, you had to have been there."

Tony rolled his eyes. "I'm glad I wasn't. The man must have hit the roof."

"Hey, what about my piano?" Laurel countered.

Instead of answering, her colleague crossed his arms and leaned back against a desk, eyeing her with renewed interest. "Did you argue like this with Nick McGraw?"

"Of course. Just because he's a famous football player and we happen to be neighbors, doesn't mean that—"

"You're neighbors?"

"Yes."

"How close?"

"Next door, but I don't see what that has to do with anything."

"Ah so, the plot thickens." He grinned as Laurel muttered a low oath and returned to her work. The plaster mix had hardened during the interim and she was forced to begin all over again.

"Don't start spreading tales," she warned. "There's absolutely nothing between us and I intend to keep it that way."

"Are you so sure about that?" He asked exactly the same question Nick had when he'd issued the challenge, Laurel realized. She wondered if men got together in locker rooms periodically to rehearse these pat little lines.

"Positive.... Why?" she tacked on suspiciously when her colleague didn't answer.

He took the X ray down and slipped it into a wide

white folder, which he tucked under his arm. "Because," he said as he left the room, "it doesn't exactly take much to see that Nick McGraw has an entirely different idea about that."

He only laughed as she threatened to throw the entire mess of soggy plaster at him.

LAUREL WAS EXHAUSTED when she pulled into her driveway much later that day. The November sun was low on the western horizon, but every bone in her body was insisting it was long past her bedtime. A quick glance next door showed that Nick's car must be in for repair. An older model Ferrari that was still a great deal more flamboyant than her American-built compact was parked in the driveway.

"What do you have against American industry?" she asked instantly as Nick opened her front door.

He braced an elbow on the doorframe, looking down at her with a puzzled expression on his face. "That's a new one. Whatever happened to 'hello dear, did you have a nice day at the office?'"

"I was referring to your choice in transportation. I've never known anyone who got an Italian sports car for a loaner."

Comprehension dawned and he grinned boyishly. "They agreed to make an exception in my case. This body would automatically reject a Plymouth."

She shook her head. "It must be nice to get everything you want out of life."

Nick neglected to tell her how far off base she was with that statement. "It's better than a jab in the eye with a sharp stick," he agreed cheerfully.

Laurel wondered why she even tried to relate to this obviously spoiled superstar. She ducked under his arm, entering her foyer.

"How's Danny?" she asked with inner trepidation. Laurel didn't know if she was up to handling tantrums and complaints this evening.

"Terrific," Nick related, following her into her living room. "He read the entire Nip the Bear book, impressing his teacher considerably, I was given to understand. Then he hit a double at recess, driving in the winning run, although he regrettably got left on third base when a less adept batter struck out. And his football has been autographed by the entire offensive line of the Phoenix Thunderbirds. As we speak I've got the kid setting the table out by the pool so we can have a picnic."

He grinned, his appraising gaze sweeping over her. "Your son, Dr. Britton, had a very good day. You, on the other hand, look about as beat up as I feel." Nick handed her a glass of chilled white wine.

"Thanks," she murmured, forgetting for the moment that she was furious with him for embarrassing her at the clinic. She took a sip of the smooth Chardonnay, finding it the perfect prescription. "Although I might point out you don't do a heck of a lot for a woman's ego, McGraw. Whatever happened to pretty compliments?"

Nick took her briefcase from her hand, tossing it down onto a pile of boxes. "I didn't think they'd work with you," he said simply.

A slight grin hovered at the corners of his mouth and Laurel noticed a scar curving up and outward from his top lip. A face mask, she decided, wondering what drove these professional athletes. It had to be more than money and fame. They suffered from their obsession far more than their fans would ever realize.

"Would they?" His deep voice broke into her thoughts.

"Would what?" she answered blankly, dragging her gaze from his firmly cut lips.

"Would pretty compliments work?"

Laurel took another sip of her wine, eyeing him silently over the rim of her glass. He'd located her dishes, she realized irrelevantly. That in itself must have been a major achievement, considering her rather haphazard packing method.

"I don't know," she answered finally. "Right now I'm so tired and discouraged that any kind word would probably seem like manna from heaven."

She was beat, Nick determined, reading the vulnerability in her eyes. Resisting the voice of conscience trying to make itself heard in the back of his mind, he closed the slight gap between them, coming to stand just inches away. Laurel drew in a breath as he reached out and tucked her dark hair behind her ear.

"I could try telling you that your hair reminds me of liquid silk. Would that appeal to your feminine ego, Laurel?"

Laurel wanted to close her eyes to the tantalizing gentle touch, but that would mean giving up viewing the bright green gaze warming her face with its darkening heat.

"It might," she murmured. "But not if you say it to every woman you meet."

"I don't. Usually the women I know have fat hair."

*And they know how to play this game,* he added silently, watching Laurel's brown eyes soften dangerously. Even with the fatigue lacing them, they were still the most alluring eyes he'd ever seen. Nick felt as if he was drowning in rich, melted chocolate.

Laurel knew encouraging such words from a man who probably considered seduction a national pastime was rash behavior. But she was powerless to move as she felt the slow, inexorable tightening of the silken web around them.

"Fat hair?"

Nick saw the movement in her throat as she swallowed. Like taking candy from a baby, he mused. She'd let her guard down and it would be so, so easy.

He lifted random strands of her glossy chestnut hair, running them through his fingers like sifting sand. "Fat hair," he repeated. "You know—three feet high, two feet wide and hard as concrete. That stuff can put a guy's eye out if he's not careful."

"Oh. Fat hair," she whispered.

The confusion in her eyes oddly failed to give him pleasure. Nick felt a flash of irritation at his uncharacteristic vacillation. This wasn't going as planned. He was creating havoc to her senses, but damn it, she wasn't supposed to be doing the same thing to him. Laurel Britton was a challenge—a lovely, desirable woman he intended to have simply because he wanted her. And Nick was used to getting everything he wanted, especially when it came to women. He frowned, annoyed by the way her liquid dark eyes created doubts that billowed in his mind like thick clouds of smoke from a prairie fire. He was frustrated, but secretly relieved as a crash from outside shattered the mood.

"Oh, my God, I completely forgot about Danny!"

"He's fine. Don't worry about him."

Laurel had broken free of the evocative mood, grateful for the flare of anger invoked by his offhanded tone. "Make up your mind, McGraw. This afternoon you questioned my mothering abilities and now you're telling me not to care when it sounds as if the house is falling down around my child's ears!"

Nick muttered a soft oath and followed her out to the brick terrace overlooking the rectangular, Grecian-style pool. Danny was fitfully sweeping up a pile of glass Laurel recognized as once having been a Waterford crystal pitcher. He paled as he looked up to see the two adults.

"Gee, mom, it just slipped out of my hands. Nick and I made some lemonade and I wanted to put it in something real special. To celebrate your first day at work." Freckles stood out vividly on his ashen complexion. "I promise I'll buy you another pitcher. I'll get a job mowing lawns after school."

Laurel's heart turned over at her son's earnest expression. She gave him an encouraging smile as she hugged him. "It was only a pitcher. Besides, in case you haven't noticed, there're not a lot of lawns around here. Everyone has desert landscaping."

"Then I'll deliver papers," he vowed, breaking away to begin his furious sweeping once again. "Or wash cars, or something. Don't worry, I'll pay you back!"

Laurel firmly extracted the broom from his hands. "Hey, kiddo, I just realized you did me a big favor by getting rid of that old thing. I never should have brought it with me."

"But that was your extra best pitcher! You've had it forever. Longer than me even."

"It was a wedding present from Grandma Britton," Laurel informed her son dryly.

Danny grimaced at the idea of the Britton family's grim-faced matriarch. "Yuck."

Laurel chuckled as she ruffled her son's hair. "My sentiments exactly. Thinking about it, I should have just given it to Amanda as a wedding present. It's more her style."

As soon as the words escaped, Laurel knew she'd made a tactical error mentioning Geoffrey's second wife. "I like Amanda, mom," Danny responded on cue.

Nick's steady green eyes were on her face as she forced a smile. "Hey, me too," she lied quickly, not about to force her child to choose sides. "It's just that since Amanda has more time to take care of things like silver and crystal, I should've given it to her in the first place."

Danny looked mollified. "I've got a great idea, mom," he said, his voice alive with youthful enthusiasm. Laurel expelled a sigh of relief they'd gotten over that touchy subject once again.

Then, unwittingly, he managed to drive a stake into her heart. "When I go home for Christmas, you can send all the fancy stuff you don't want back with me."

Feeling Nick's curious study of her stricken expression, Laurel knelt, keeping her head down as she picked up the larger shards of crystal. Ever since discovering her own infertility, Amanda had been pressuring Geoffrey to talk Laurel into allowing Danny to live with them. Laurel knew her ex-husband had no real wish to have his son with him full-time, but if it made his wife happy, he'd certainly give it his best shot. While he hadn't yet gone as far as suing for custody, Laurel suspected he and Amanda were planning to convince Danny during his Christmas visit that he'd be happier in Seattle.

She had to force her answer past the lump in her throat. "Good idea, Danny. Do you have any of that lemonade left?" When he nodded, she suggested with feigned brightness, "Why don't you go fill a plastic pitcher this time and bring it out?"

Her eyes were burning with unshed tears as she turned away from Nick's observant gaze. "Home," she murmured, as if to herself. "Of course he still thinks of Seattle as home."

Nick knew Laurel was hurting and wondered at the cause. It had to be more than the fact Danny was suffering from normal homesickness. He wondered how long Laurel had been divorced. Had her husband left her for this Amanda person? Was she still carrying a torch for him? Was she here in Phoenix because, unable to watch her ex-husband basking in connubial bliss with his new wife, she'd run away? That idea caused an oddly unpleasant feeling of jealousy that he forced away.

He came up behind her, cupping her slumped shoulders in his strong palms. "Hey, that's only natural. The kid's lived there all his life. Give it some time, Laurel."

She sniffled inelegantly, wiping at the traitorous tears with the back of her hand. "I know all that, intellectually. Damn. You must think I'm an absolute idiot."

Forgetting for the moment his desire to get her into his bed, Nick only wanted to comfort. "No, I think you're dead on your feet," he corrected calmly. "Just wait until you get Dr. McGraw's famous, fast-acting, pleasant-tasting, secret formula for weary bodies and aching bones. It's guaranteed to cure all ills that dare to plague beautiful, sexy women physicians."

Laurel managed a shaky laugh at his encouraging tone. "I'm afraid to ask."

"Do you like gourmet Italian fare, milady?"

"You're kidding!"

"Of course I'm not," he countered, an expression of mock affront on his tanned face. "In fact, even as we speak, the finest Italian chefs are working their fingers to the bone preparing a feast that'll make your lusciously attractive mouth water."

His eyes danced with a devilish gleam that reminded Laurel of Danny's, when he'd gotten into mischief.

"I think you've just slipped the bonds of maturity once again, McGraw," she accused lightly. "Why do

I get the feeling there's more to this than meets the eye?''

At that moment, as if on cue, Danny reappeared, supplying her answer. "Hey, Nick, I need twenty dollars. The guy's here with the pizzas.''

"Gourmet?'' She arched a dark eyebrow.

Nick shrugged, digging into his back pocket for his wallet. "Hey, don't worry your pretty little head about it. I spare no expense when it comes to my friends.''

He grinned, ruffling her hair with the same easy familiarity she had Danny's. "Take your shoes off and sit down, Dr. Britton,'' he prescribed over his shoulder as he left to pay the delivery man. "Dinner is served.''

Laurel was amazed they got through the meal without a single argument, or a repeat of that disturbing sensuality that settled over them from time to time. Danny talked a mile a minute, his words coming like machine-gun fire as he told her all about his day. It was easy to tell the high point had been the Thunderbirds' practice.

"Hey, mom,'' he offered into a moment of comfortable silence. "You should've seen Nick! He got sacked on the last play and still ran wind sprints after scrimmage.''

The wedge of gooey pizza had been on the way to her mouth but at Danny's admiring statement she slowly lowered it to her plate. Her gaze cut to Nick's impassive face.

"Since when is the quarterback fair game in scrimmages?''

He shrugged with exaggerated nonchalance. "Since Carr took over as coach. His feeling is that they hit quarterbacks in the game, why not in practice?''

Laurel stared at him, waiting to hear it was

merely his idea of a bad joke. "You've got to be kidding."

He wished he was. "Nope. The day of putting a red jersey on a quarterback that says 'don't hit this poor bastard' is over, I guess. At least as far as the Thunderbirds go."

"That knee of yours can't take that many hits," she said sharply. "It's criminal that your own coach is allowing such behavior. Encouraging it, even."

He waved a dismissive hand, casting a quick glance toward Danny, who was watching the exchange with avid interest. "Hey, don't worry about it. I can still take a few hits, can't I, sport?"

Danny nodded vigorously, his mouth filled with pizza. His eyes were bright with obvious hero worship and Laurel knew that as his physician, she and Nick were going to have to discuss this seriously. But he was right. There was no point in worrying her son.

"Wind sprints?" she asked under her breath as Danny took off toward the gate, carrying a thick slice of pepperoni pizza to Rowdy, who'd been whining on his side of the fence.

"You'd better believe it," Nick groaned, dropping his macho pose for the moment. "Three-and-a-half miles of forty-yard dashes."

"I'm not allowing that!"

He managed a wry grin. "What am I supposed to do? Bring a note from my neighbor?"

She crossed her arms over her chest. "No—from your doctor. You're in danger of causing permanent injury to that knee, Nick McGraw. I can't believe you'd take a stupid risk like that."

"I've got to play, Laurel. And I'll put up with whatever Carr tries to force me off the team rather than quit." His expression grew momentarily fierce. "Hell, I know the message he's sending. He's letting me know that while I may admittedly be the star, he pulls the strings. It's just a power play with some guys.''

Nick was amazed as Laurel cursed him fluently, her tone low in deference to her son, but her words extremely colorful and as imaginative as any he'd heard.

''Is that any way to talk to your poor wounded patient?'' he objected. ''Don't tell me they taught you that language in medical school, Dr. Britton.''

She glared at him, finding the amusement in his green eyes even more maddening than his devil-may-care attitude about his safety.

''This isn't funny,'' she snapped.

His gaze turned solemn. ''I never said it was.''

Nick sighed, rising from his chair to pace back and forth in silent aggravation. Laurel couldn't help noticing the pronounced limp that hadn't been there earlier that day when she'd examined him.

Her tone was measurably softer, coaxing compliance this time, rather than demanding obedience. ''At least sit down.''

He did as requested, flinging his body onto a lounge chair. Linking his fingers together behind his head, he closed his eyes for a long, thoughtful time.

Free to study him openly, Laurel detected definite signs of fatigue she'd not noticed earlier. Weary from the unexpected patient load, trying to learn unfamiliar office procedures and putting up with Dr. Adams's uncordial attitude, she hadn't considered the possibility that Nick would be every bit as exhausted as she. More so, she amended, considering the outrageous practice he'd undergone.

She rose slowly, moving to sit on the edge of the lounge. ''I've an idea,'' she suggested softly. ''Why don't I give you a massage and you can get to bed? I've been a selfish rat letting you take care of Danny and provide dinner, too.... See what happens to people who volunteer? They get taken advantage of."

His eyes remained shut. "It was only pizza."

She smiled and Nick could hear it in her voice. "It sure tasted like gourmet Italian cooking to me, McGraw. I was so starved I would've settled for the box it came in."

He opened his eyes at that, sharing the smile with her. As their gazes locked, he found his exhaustion being rapidly replaced by a familiar, escalating desire.

"Who's suggesting that massage? Dr. Britton, or her lovely alter ego, Laurel?"

The message in Nick's deep velvety voice was unmistakable and Laurel had to fight against every rebellious atom in her body as she forced a casual tone. "Sorry, Mr. Football Star, but that offer came from Dr. Britton."

He trailed a finger up her arm. "I know why you're doing this, Laurel."

"Doing what?"

"Taking care of me like this."

"I'm your doctor," she reminded him, as well as herself.

His gaze was bright with insinuation. "True, but there's another reason you're not being honest enough to admit."

"Oh, really?" Her voice was unsteady as the treacherous finger traced a line along her collarbone. Dear God, it was happening again.

He winked a brilliant emerald eye. "Of course. You need help unpacking all those crates and I wouldn't be of much use hobbling around on a pair of crutches, now would I?"

Laurel didn't return his teasing smile this time. "If you're not careful, you'll end up in far worse shape than that."

He shook his blond head. "Laurel, Laurel," he said on a deep sigh. "Didn't I tell you not to sweat the little stuff?"

"Nick—"

"Now hush, woman. I don't want to disillusion what may be my last remaining fan."

He looked over her shoulder at Danny, who was returning from feeding the dog. Laurel bit off her frustrated response, forced to save her argument for later.

Danny's broad grin claimed his freckled face. "Rowdy's a great dog, Nick."

"I've always thought so. But he gets awfully lonely now that I'm back at work. I don't suppose you'd be willing to help me out with that little problem?" he asked casually.

Laurel watched her son's eyes light with hopeful anticipation. "Sure. But how?"

Nick sat up, swinging his feet to the ground. "This battered old body isn't as spry as it used to be. Especially after daily practice. Rowdy needs someone younger to play fetch, swim with him, spend a little time with him each evening. You wouldn't know anyone willing to do that, would you?"

"I would!"

"And of course I'll pay you," Nick tacked on.

"Wow! Did you hear that, mom?"

"I heard it, but you certainly can't take any money for playing with Nick's dog, Daniel Britton, so get that gleam of avarice out of your eyes."

"He wouldn't be playing, Laurel," Nick argued smoothly. "He'd be exercising Rowdy for me." His eyes shone devilishly. "Unless you think a nightly jog with my dog would be good for my knees."

"Of course not," she snapped, wishing he'd take his situation more seriously.

Nick rubbed his hands together, grinning with

obvious satisfaction. "Then it's a deal. A dollar a day, and all the lemonade you can drink."

Danny looked as if he'd just been given the assignment to search for the Holy Grail. "Wow," he repeated once again. "It's a deal. And I promise never to miss a day!"

Nick laughed and Laurel managed a tentative smile as Danny began talking about the practice once again. The conversation turned to anecdotes about games played during Nick's long professional career, and as the last faint color of day tinged the sky a brilliant scarlet and gold, Danny's lashes began to drift closed.

"He's had an exciting day," she murmured. "I think it's time for him to go to bed."

"Need some help?" he inquired as Danny's head settled into the curve of her shoulder.

"No, I can handle it. Why don't you pour us some more wine and I'll be back out to give you that massage I promised."

He sighed happily. "Wine, a lovely lady and a massage, all in one night. I'm not certain I can handle that much happiness, Laurel."

"You're tough, McGraw. Believe me, you'll survive."

The answering smile faded from Nick's face as he watched her leave. He lay back on the lounge, attempting to sort out these inexplicable feelings for Laurel he kept experiencing.

He couldn't say he'd been instantly drawn to her. That would be a lie. Yet, from the moment she'd begun arguing about that ridiculous excuse for a piano, he'd felt a certain unwilling admiration for her behavior. Good old-fashioned spunk was what his father would call it, he knew.

He empathized with the way her life had suddenly altered and knew how wearisome and oftentimes frightening it was to adapt to change. He hadn't handled his own life well this past year. Nick hoped he could salvage the situation by regaining his ranking as one of the top three quarterbacks in the country. Although he was no longer capable of scrambling the intricate patterns that had earned the Thunderbirds three trips to the Super Bowl and two national titles, he could still pass. And if he had to put up with all Carr's marine-sergeant drills to get back on top, then so be it.

He liked the way Laurel seemed honestly concerned about him and sensed her worry came as much from the woman as the doctor. He certainly wasn't used to genuine concern. Most women gushed over him when he'd first been injured, but he'd always known that the first Sunday he couldn't drag himself out onto the field, the crowd of willing admiring females would disappear. They were along for the ride, and it was understood they wouldn't be expected to tag along if it took a downhill turn anywhere along the way.

Laurel was the flip side of that coin. Nick expected one hell of an argument about his practice routines. He could practically see her storming onto the field, giving Coach Ward Carr a piece of her mind. That was something he was going to have to make certain didn't happen, if he had to tie her up and sit on her.

"Something funny?"

She'd returned and was standing over him, a puzzled expression on her face. Nick realized he'd been smiling at the thought of holding the feisty Dr. Britton down anywhere against her will.

"I was considering the logistics of holding you down when you'd made up your mind to do something," he admitted.

Laurel didn't mince words. "Like telling that idiot

who's masquerading as a football coach what I think of live hitting in his damn scrimmages?''

Nick knew the anger flashing in her dark eyes was not meant for him. He patted the lounge, inviting her to sit down. ''That was one of the more unwelcome scenarios.''

''I don't know if you understand how important it is for you to go slowly, Nick.''

His level gaze held hers. ''And I'm not certain you understand how important it is for me to make a full comeback this season.''

She realized he was actually going to jeopardize his knee in order to continue playing. It was times like this she wanted to pick up the nearest thing and knock some sense into these obsessive athletes. Laurel ran—every day as a rule—but she'd never behaved as if it was the only thing in her life.

She rose from the lounge in an abrupt, jerky movement, wrapping her arms about herself as she walked to the edge of the pool. They'd turned on the underwater light earlier in the evening, making the water gleam a bright, welcoming aquamarine. But her mind was not on the inviting depths. Instead she was seeing Nick's torn and battered knee.

''If you're insisting on miracle cures, you've got the wrong doctor, McGraw. Try signing on a faith healer instead. Because I don't have anything to offer.''

*Oh yes, you do, lovely Laurel,* he could have answered. He still wanted her. His fingertips tingled with the need to experience the satin of her skin and he knew he'd go crazy if he couldn't taste of those luscious ripe lips soon. Nick tilted back his head, tossing off the rest of his wine. He couldn't remember when he'd wanted—needed—a woman more.

Although he was vaguely disturbed by the fact Laurel had already affected him more deeply than other women of his experience, Nick refused to allow himself to worry. If things became too difficult, he could always solve this dilemma by getting up, walking through that gate and remaining forever on his own side of the fence. He knew that with an ironclad certainty. Just as he knew he wasn't going to do it.

"I THOUGHT WE'D agreed to be friends," Nick said simply.

Laurel didn't turn around. "We agreed to *try* being friends. But it isn't going to work; you're too hardheaded."

"And you're not?"

Laurel sighed, slowly turning toward him. Her distress was written all over her face. "Of course I am. But I'm your doctor and you refuse to listen to me!"

He rose, gingerly favoring his right leg as he came to stand in front of her. Only a few inches separated them as he gazed down, his eyes caressing her face.

"You're also an attractive woman, Laurel. And I've listened to every word you've said."

His thumb moved lightly up her throat, tracing the line of her slender jaw, coming to rest at the corner of her lips.

"You have such a beautiful mouth," he murmured, his square-cut thumbnail following the full upper arch of her top lip. "It just begs to be kissed."

"Now you're being fanciful," she whispered, trembling slightly at the feathery touch against her skin.

"No, I'm not," he corrected firmly, but gently. "Tell me the truth, haven't you been wondering all day what this kiss would be like?"

To her dismay, Laurel found herself incapable of denying his words. "It's only a natural curiosity," she finally said softly, trying to explain away these sensations. Every time she considered the idea of

Nick McGraw's firm lips pressing against hers, she felt as if she'd been buffeted by a brisk autumn wind.

"Only natural," he agreed. "And since we're both adults, there's really no harm in satisfying a totally normal curiosity."

"So long as it's only a kiss, I suppose no harm could come of it. Since we're both adults," she echoed on a whisper.

His eyes moved across her face with the intensity of a physical caress as his thumb toyed at the corner of her lips. Laurel felt her mouth go suddenly dry and as she nervously licked her lips, Nick stifled a deep masculine groan.

"I'm going to kiss you now, Laurel," he warned her with great gravity.

Her softly-lit dark eyes gave him her answer as Laurel swallowed again, watching Nick's sun-streaked head come closer. She closed her eyes, breathing in the enticing scent of his after-shave. Green, she decided, like a forest, but not a brisk pine. It was warm and primeval. Blending with Nick's own masculine scent, the aroma was of moist dark earth—pungent, heady and so very, very right for him.

As his mouth touched hers lightly, she thought, *I shouldn't be doing this.* Not with this man. Definitely not with this man, she repeated even while delighting in the mint-sprigged taste of his breath.

Nick's fingers cupped her jaw, not moving to explore her body as they experienced how thrilling a mere kiss can be when two people come together at that perfect moment in time. His lips plucked at hers, tenderly, teasingly, and as they blazed a trail over her uptilted face, leaving sparks on every inch of heated skin—her eyelids, her cheeks, her temple, her chin—Laurel knew this kiss surpassed any that might have come before it.

"Nice," he murmured, his teeth nibbling with gentle beguilement on her earlobe.

"Very nice," she agreed on a soft sound of pleasure.

"Shall we try again?"

She knew she was playing with fire, but like a moth drawn to a flame, she couldn't resist the gleaming warmth in his eyes.

"I still have a little bit of curiosity left," she admitted, her melted-chocolate gaze handing him a clear invitation.

"I'm giving you fair warning, sweetheart. All this is piquing mine even more." His voice was gruff, unmistakably laced with bridled passion.

Laurel couldn't remember moving, but a moment later she was folded in his arms. "This is madness," she murmured, a faint tinge of regret in her tone.

"Mmm," he said. "Let's hear it for the loonies. They really know how to live."

A slow kindling longing was building up inside Laurel as her breasts yielded softly to the strength of his chest and she gave herself up to the absolute glory of his kiss, knowing that if this was indeed madness, she didn't know why sanity had always been held up as the ideal.

Degree by glorious degree he deepened the kiss, and Laurel willingly responded, her lips hungry under his. The rest of the world slipped away as her attention centered solely on Nick's lips. Lips that were continually changing, first hard and strong, then soft and gentle. And sweet, so wonderfully, dazzlingly sweet. It was as if he meant to kiss her endlessly, and as his lips became the center of her universe, the sun of her existence, Laurel prayed he'd never stop.

"Well?"

His deep voice sliced through the sensual fog of

her thoughts and Laurel's eyes flew open to view Nick observing her with an inordinate amount of outward calm.

She did her best to match it, not wanting him to know she had been taken to the very edge of reason with a mere kiss.

"I'd say my curiosity has been satisfied. You're a very good kisser, Nick. But I suppose it's like everything else—practice makes perfect."

Nick forced his attention away from the fire surging through his veins. He wanted to be alone with Laurel; he wanted to explore her satiny skin at his leisure, to taste and touch and experience every inch of her slender, perfect body. Need vibrated through him even as his mind attempted to make sense of the fact this woman had succeeded in turning his world upside down with only a kiss.

"It helps," he agreed cheerfully. Lord, he didn't want to ever let her go. "Want to practice together?"

Laurel knew if she allowed an encore of that performance, she'd be an absolute goner. Besides, a faint little voice of reason was trying to make itself heard in the distant pockets of her mind. It was telling her this was a far cry from a professional patient-doctor relationship.

She pressed against the rock-hard strength of his shoulders. "I'd say we've satisfied our curiosity, Nick. Let's leave it at that."

At her crisp, professional tone, Nick wondered if Dr. Laurel Britton was actually capable of such iron-clad control. Impossible. She was, however, a hell of an actress. He struggled to maintain an appearance of nonchalance, deciding to allow her this retreat for the time being.

While he was definitely not a patient man, Nick knew that by not forcing the issue, his eventual victory would be even sweeter. She wanted him; everything from her softly glazed dark eyes to her trembling as she'd pressed her willowy body against his gave her away. It was only a matter of time.

"It's probably just as well," he said lightly. "You'd just let slip what a magnificent lover I was to one of your girlfriends, and I'd have to sell my house, change my name and move to another town in order to get any rest."

"Your ego is as fat as your medical chart, McGraw," Laurel said with a laugh, relieved by his easy acceptance and enjoying his good humor.

She'd been afraid she was going to have a fight on her hands and cool waves of relief rushed over her as she slipped out of the circle of his arms and began gathering up paper plates and glasses.

"Hey, what are you doing?"

"Cleaning up so I can get to sleep. I work, remember?"

"What about my massage?"

Laurel recognized determination when she saw it, possessing a fair share of that personality trait herself. Nick McGraw wanted her, and if she was to be perfectly honest, she'd have to admit he wasn't alone in his desire. But Laurel also knew their mutual attraction was far too dangerous. To get involved with this man would be like strapping sticks of TNT to her body and walking into a roomful of pyromaniacs armed with matches. It was only a passing infatuation, she assured herself. Just avoid temptation and it would run its natural course.

"I've already massaged that oversize male ego by admitting you're a pretty fair kisser, Nick. Let's save the body for some other night."

She was definitely shaken. Nick gave himself points as he stood his ground, his grin surprisingly boyish. "Promise?"

Laurel sought refuge in her profession. "Do you

promise to take it easy during practice?" she countered.

"I promise to hit the deck every time I see a human mountain heading my way."

Her expression was one of genuine concern. "Do you swear? No heroics?"

He lifted a palm in the gesture of a pledge. "No unnecessary heroics," he agreed.

Laurel's breath escaped on a rippling sigh. It was impossible not to catch his alteration of her request. "Go home, McGraw. I've had about as much of you as I can take for one day."

Nick was not used to receiving such dismissal from anyone, let alone a woman. He'd discovered at the early age of twelve his extraordinary talent with a football caused people to cater to him, granting his every wish. Fawning females had never irritated him; on the contrary, he'd taken their presence as his natural right. He was a star, and it only made sense that as such, he received preferential treatment.

But if Laurel was the type of woman to pay homage to any man, he'd yet to see any indication of such forthcoming behavior. She'd teased him, argued with him and steadfastly refused him. She'd also intrigued him. Even as badly as he wanted her body, Nick found himself wanting to know this woman better. He was determined to stay close to her until all his curiosity about the lovely Dr. Laurel Britton was finally satisfied.

"May I pick Danny up from school again tomorrow?"

Laurel shook her head slowly. *Keep him at a distance,* she warned herself firmly. "I don't think so. I don't want him to get used to spending every evening with you."

"Hey, I didn't say anything about the evening."

His crooked grin was mildly apologetic as he glibly thought up the lie. "As it happens, I've got a date tomorrow night. I was going to suggest you could pick him up at the field after you finish at the clinic. Practice won't be over until about six."

Laurel fought against revealing the disappointment his words caused. Of course there would be a plethora of women in this man's life, what did she expect?

"Oh. Then I suppose it's all right. If you're certain he's no bother."

"None at all. I like kids, believe it or not. Even ones who root for the Seahawks." His smile extended to his eyes. "Good night, Laurel."

"Good night, Nick," she murmured, lifting her hand in farewell as he disappeared through the gate.

She finished cleaning up, then undressed, flinging her clothing in a careless trail behind her as she made her way through the maze of unpacked cartons to the master bedroom. As she slid beneath the sheet emblazoned with rainbows, it crossed Laurel's mind that not in the three years since her divorce, had this king-size bed ever seemed so lonely. Then, exhausted, she gave herself up to a much needed sleep.

LAUREL'S SECOND DAY at the clinic proved less stressful than the first. Now that the rash of holiday injuries had passed, her patient load was far more manageable, and she found herself falling into the routine as if she'd been there for months, and not just two days. The only fly in the ointment, she considered with wry resignation, was Dr. Adams. Continually during the day she felt those steely gray eyes watching her, observing her silently, as if waiting for a misstep. He did, however, refrain from entering into direct confrontation.

"Hey, you look great," Tony Lee complimented her as she exited the women's lounge after freshening up at the end of the day. "Hot date tonight?"

Laurel self-consciously smoothed nonexistent wrinkles from her cream linen skirt. "Not at all. In fact, I'm unpacking tonight."

Her colleague's dark eyes danced devilishly. "I see. And you always dress up like that for manual labor."

"I'm not dressed up. For heaven's sake, it's the same outfit I've worn all day."

His observant gaze moved judiciously from the top of her head, taking in her freshly brushed dark hair, down to her toes. "You weren't wearing high heels," he pointed out.

She shrugged. "Flats are more practical for work."

He nodded solemnly. "Of course. Just like heels are more practical for unpacking moving crates." A teasing grin quirked at the corner of his lips. "You've also unfastened an additional button on that enticing silk blouse you kept unkindly covered by a starched lab coat all day. And the seductive cloud of fragrance hovering about you is definitely not antiseptic, Dr. Britton."

Before she could come up with an appropriate answer to Tony's all-too-accurate observation, Dr. Adams stopped by on his way to the parking lot.

"Doing a little trolling this evening, Dr. Britton?"

"Excuse me?"

For an instant, Laurel thought she detected a glimmer of interest in the man's cold eyes as they flicked over her. "Bait, Dr. Britton, obviously bait. If that football player responds to White Shoulders, I'd say you're going to land a big one tonight." With that, he walked away.

Laurel watched him go, shaking her head in genuine confusion. "I cannot figure that man out."

She turned toward Tony. "Did you get the odd impression that... Oh, skip it, that's ridiculous."

"That our illustrious administrator displayed a moment of honest masculine appreciation before slipping back behind his carp mask?"

Laurel was sorry she'd brought it up. She was not one to dig for masculine compliments, nor was it usual behavior to go out of her way to appear attractive to one certain man as she admittedly had this evening.

"I told you it was ridiculous."

"Of course it's not," Tony countered swiftly. "If I wasn't happily married, I'd be hoping you'd gone to that much trouble for me." His teasing grin appeared playfully expectant. "You didn't, did you?"

"Do you want to lock up or shall I?" she countered abruptly, changing the subject.

Tony shoved his hands into his pockets, knowing when to give up. "You go on ahead, Laurel. I'll take care of things. And hey, have a nice evening." When she looked at him sharply, he gave her an expression of sheer innocence. "With your unpacking."

Laurel's nervousness increased as she drove to the Phoenix Thunderbirds' practice field. Would Nick notice she'd gone out of her way to appear feminine and appealing? Would he realize that although she disliked admitting it, even to herself, she'd dressed with him in mind?

"Of course he will, dummy," she muttered as she idled her compact car at a red light. "Even Adams noticed. And I'll bet my little black bag it's been years since any life stirred in that man's icy blue blood."

The thought of her acrimonious superior made her scowl at the same time her attention shifted toward the car next to her. The middle-aged man had been eyeing her with friendly interest, but at her blistering gaze, a dark red flush rose from his collar and he quickly swiveled his head toward the windshield. Laurel sighed, shifting gears as the light changed and she made her way through the intersection.

She spotted Danny right away at the field, and as she walked along the sidelines to where he waited behind the Thunderbirds' bench, her appearance drew a few admiring whistles. While she managed to keep her head high and her eyes straight ahead, Laurel secretly admitted the attention was rather nice.

A roar rose from the spectators and she stopped momentarily to watch the action on the field. Although it was November and early evening, the unseasonable temperature was in the high nineties. She was surprised to see the players practicing in full gear.

Nick took the snap from the center, dropped back and scanned the coverage. She cringed, hoping he wouldn't swivel too abruptly and put too much pressure on his damaged knee, but as it turned out, he didn't have time. A linebacker the size of an enormous sequoia broke through the offensive line and Nick vanished under an avalanche of bodies. The watching fans breathed the united sound a crowd makes while watching Fourth of July fireworks. Then to Laurel's amazement, they began to applaud.

It was all she could do to keep from running out on the field, both the doctor and the woman in her aghast at the intensity of the hit. She pressed her fingers against her lips, forcing herself to wait.

A murmur ran through the ranks as Nick rose to his feet, apparently unharmed. But Laurel knew that if practices continued at this level, it would be a miracle if he made it all the way through the season.

"Isn't that a pretty hard tackle for a scrimmage, coach?"

She turned in the direction of the question, observing the television camera on the sidelines focused on the short, stocky coach.

Ward Carr pushed his Thunderbirds cap back on his head. "Hell, football is a tough game. A violent game. No cream puffs need apply," he replied in a gravelly, rough voice.

"Are you calling Nick McGraw a cream puff?" the sportscaster asked on a note of disbelief.

"Look, in this sport pain is just a state of mind. I'm no doctor—if McGraw says he's ready to play, then he damn well better be ready to get hit. Every player knows he's going to get hurt, and the chances are he could get hurt bad. If a guy can't take it, let him get the hell out of the game. That's football. We intend to make winners out of these guys if we have to do it over their dead bodies."

His tone was casual, even flippant, and Laurel felt her temper escalating to dangerous proportions. The man was an absolute menace. She was on the verge of telling him exactly that, on television if possible, when she felt a hand tugging at the sleeve of her blouse.

"Hi, mom. Isn't it nifty?"

"It's criminal," she answered, raising her voice to a level she hoped would be picked up by the microphone. Her furious gaze held Ward Carr's as well as that of the surprised sportscaster, who glanced back over his shoulder to see who was interfering with his taped interview. "This kind of rough practice is ridiculous at the professional level."

She heard Carr mumble something under his breath, earning an appreciative laugh from the sportscaster as they returned their attention to the subject at hand. Laurel fumed silently, glancing toward the field just in time to see Nick complete a short, hard pass.

"Can we stay a little longer, mom? They're almost finished."

She knew watching the vicious scrimmage would only aggravate her further. But the sight of Nick, clad in a red-and-gold jersey, held an unwilling fascination.

"Just a bit," she agreed. "We've a lot to do at home, though. We can't keep living like Gypsies."

"Gee, thanks mom. You're the greatest!" His freckled face was wreathed in a smile and Laurel said a silent prayer Danny would remember that at Christmas, when he was back with his father in Seattle.

She agonized during the next half hour as the practice became even more vicious and the pileups deepened. The assistant coaches had obviously been instructed to hold their whistle-blowing to a minimum, and fistfights were becoming almost routine after every play. One particularly savage hit drove Nick into a group of players watching from behind the line of scrimmage, stretching him out flat on the turf. She was distressed but not surprised when he came up swinging at the offending linebacker, and the players had to separate these opposing members of the same team.

That was fortunately the last play of the day, and after an incredible series of wind sprints, the players were allowed to limp their way to the showers. Instead of leaving the field immediately, Nick came toward her, waving his gold helmet in his hand.

"Are you all right?" Her worried brown eyes skimmed his body, as if searching for injuries before focusing on his face.

He shrugged, reaching out to tousle Danny's hair. "Just a nice, light workout for an autumn evening. You look terrific, by the way, Dr. Britton. And don't tell me that's Phisohex."

Laurel smiled. "No," she admitted. "White Shoulders."

"My favorite kind."

"Perfume?"

"That, too."

He grinned, his teasing gaze moving over her amber silk blouse, as he envisioned her pearly skin underneath. She'd gone out of her way to leave Dr. Britton back at the clinic, he determined. This luscious lady was definitely the lovely Laurel. Oh no, they weren't finished. Not by a long shot.

Laurel could feel the silken web settling over them once again and was relieved when Danny broke the evocative silence.

"Can I come again tomorrow, mom?"

She looked from her son to Nick. "I don't know."

Nick shrugged, his shoulders appearing even more massive in the wide shoulder pads. "It's okay with me, Laurel."

"We'll talk about it when we get home, Danny," she hedged, taking his hand as she nodded to Nick. "I think you'd better put some ice on that elbow, Nick. It looked as if you jarred it when you were hit that last time."

His eyes were glued to her mouth. 'Yeah, I did," he answered absently. As she appeared ready to leave, he had to fight back the urge to reach out and touch her. "Hey, want me to walk you and Danny out to your car?"

Laurel shook her head, keeping her regret from showing on her face. "No. You'd better get showered and changed. You'll be late for your date."

As Nick watched Laurel walk away, her back straight, her stride long and purposeful, he had an overwhelming urge to shout out for her to stop.

# 5

LAUREL TRIED HER BEST to stop her imagination from conjuring up such vivid pictures of what Nick was doing on his date while the evening progressed. She threw herself into her work, determined to make some inroads into the herculean task before her. Making her way through the kitchen boxes first, she vowed to go shopping during her lunch break tomorrow and buy some nutritious food. While she knew Danny would happily continue eating takeout for the rest of his life, she felt guilty about not providing him with home-cooked, well-balanced meals.

By midnight she'd emptied all the crates in the kitchen, dining room and living room. Danny had been sound asleep for hours, and she went upstairs to take a shower, scrubbing at the newsprint stains on her skin. As she rubbed herself dry with a soft terry towel, Laurel couldn't help fantasizing the touch of Nick's wide, strong hands.

What was he doing now, she wondered, clutching the towel to her breasts. Was he lying with some voluptuous blonde, his lips and fingertips caressing every lush curve? She allowed the towel to drop unheeded to the floor, her judicious gaze taking in her reflection in the full-length mirror.

"You're too skinny for a man like him," she murmured, knowing while her uptilted breasts were firm, she'd never have a photographer from *Playboy* banging on her door. She splayed her fingers on her waist, giving herself credit for its narrow span. However, as her hands traced her hips, Laurel admitted that while she could be considered boyishly attractive in jeans, her curves would never inspire erotic fantasies in a man with the ready-made harem Nick McGraw probably possessed.

Her legs were long, her thighs firm from running, the well-defined curve of her calves leading to trim ankles. "Maybe he's an ankle man," she mused, wondering if she had the nerve to go out and buy one of those slim gold chains to see if it would garner Nick's attention.

She shook herself firmly back to reality, pulling her short blue robe from a hook on the back of the bathroom door. "That idea is ridiculous for a woman of your age," she scolded herself firmly. "Next you'll be thinking of putting a ruby in your navel and wearing crimson harem pants. Physicians do not dress like belly dancers." She marched out of the bathroom, flicking off the light behind her. "And they definitely don't fantasize about making love with their patients!"

Still irritatingly wide-awake, Laurel wandered into the kitchen to make herself a cup of hot chocolate, hoping it would help her sleep. She couldn't keep herself from glancing out the window. It had begun to rain, and through the slanting drops she saw a few random lights on in Nick's house. Was he home? Was he in one of those darkened rooms, lying in a passionate embrace, his masculine appetites temporarily satiated?

Laurel groaned, unwilling to submit herself to any further mental torture. She dragged her gaze downward to the pan of milk, determinedly watching for the little ring of bubbles. Moments later, a knock at the kitchen door startled her.

"Nick!" She stared up at him as he opened the door.

"Hi. I saw your light and thought you might not

mind some company." He leaned against her door-frame, smiling down at her as if he saw nothing un-usual about dropping in at this late hour.

In truth, he'd had to force himself to wait this long. Now, in retrospect, he was glad he'd waited. Her flushed, freshly bathed skin exuded a faint, in-toxicating fragrance that weakened his knees. Then Nick belatedly realized he hadn't come up with an excuse for coming over here. He couldn't allow her to think his only motive had been the simple need to see her again.

"I thought you might like a little help with your unpacking," he ad-libbed the lie.

*This can't become a habit*, she told herself firmly. *If you let him come over here after dates like this, you're only going to end up getting hurt.*

"I was just going to bed," she lied badly, her fingers gripping the edges of her short satin robe a little closer together. From the gleam that suddenly lit his eyes, Laurel knew he'd perceived she was wearing nothing under the robe.

Nick feigned absolute innocence, directing his gaze past her shoulder. "Your milk's burning."

"Oh damn!" Laurel spun around, taking the pan from the heat and dumping the caramelized remains down the drain.

"Let me," he suggested. "I make a hell of a cup of cocoa."

"You?" She arched a challenging eyebrow. "I find that extremely difficult to believe."

"Why?"

"I just can't imagine you being handy in the kitchen."

His green eyes gleamed with a provocative mes-sage. "Oh, I don't know, I've been assured that I'm pretty handy all over the house." He allowed a long, wicked pause. "Want me to audition?"

Her gaze narrowed as she held the lapels of her robe more tightly together. The increased beat of her heart thumped wildly in her ears and Laurel irrationally worried Nick could hear it as well.

"We're talking cocoa here, right?"

"Of course. From scratch, actually," he stated calmly, eyeing her instant hot chocolate mix with a frown. He dug around in her cupboard, pulling things out and lining them up on the counter. "Let's see, cocoa, sugar, salt, a little vanilla, cinnamon. You're going to love this."

Unfortunately, Laurel believed him. She tried to find something about the man she didn't like. "What happened to your date?" she asked caustically. "Did the great Nick McGraw strike out?"

"That's baseball. And I never kiss and tell."

"A casanova with principles. Will wonders never cease."

He grinned as he observed her over his shoulder. "Ouch. 'They have sharpened their tongues like a snake.'"

"Is that Shakespeare?" she inquired, wishing her premed studies had allowed more of an acquaintance with liberal arts.

Laurel always felt uneasy with people who could spout clever quotations. It was certainly not that she was undereducated; she'd just never found any way to fit the structure of the DNA molecule into casual conversation.

"Nope. The Bible. Psalms." He was stirring the mixture and missed her incredulous gaze.

"A casanova who quotes Psalms? Now that *is* unique."

"I'm one in a million," he agreed cheerfully, reaching into a cupboard and taking down two handcrafted ceramic mugs. Laurel watched the little spiral of steam rise as he poured the dark chocolate mixture.

"Here, try this."

She lifted the bright, flowered mug to her lips, taking a tentative sip. It was rich, sweet and a definite improvement over the uninspired drink she'd been going to make.

"You're hired," she said immediately.

Nick chuckled, pulling up a chair and straddling it, folding his arms along the top. "Why do I have a feeling that while you are probably one terrific Dr. Frankenstein in the laboratory, you're not that comfortable in the kitchen?"

"I've been known to burn water," she admitted. "Fortunately Danny has simple tastes. His father finally gave up on my culinary efforts and ate at the hospital." She managed a wry grin. "If you've ever tasted institutional food, that gives you some indication of my questionable abilities in the kitchen."

Nick's gaze was as warm as Laurel's cocoa. "I think you're underestimating yourself," he murmured, his eyes moving over her face with the impact of a physical caress. "I'm sure you're marvelous in the kitchen. In the bathroom. In the bedroom, and—"

"Nick." She cut him off with a shaky note of warning.

"Spoilsport."

His smile was masculinely challenging as he eyed her over the top of his mug. When he patted his lips with a paper napkin, Laurel wondered why she should find that simple gesture so provocative. She focused on those firmly cut lips and her blood warmed at the memory of the feel of them against her own.

Nick didn't miss the rosy flush under her skin, but he forced himself to keep the conversation casual. For now.

"Danny's father is a doctor, too?"

Laurel nodded.

"Sports?"

That earned a bitter laugh. "Hardly."

"Something less than honorable in treating jocks?" he asked curiously.

Nick had to fight to keep his eyes on her face. Her robe had parted just enough to allow an entrancing view of silky skin and he longed for the opportunity to view Laurel's slender body at his leisure. White Shoulders fit her perfectly, he decided, stealing a surreptitious glance at her creamy flesh.

"No, it's just that Geoffrey chose a specialty more suited to his image of himself as a healer. He's a cardiovascular surgeon. He feels it inspires more awe than general practitioners taking care of runny noses, or sports specialists taping up swollen ankles."

"I suppose I can understand that. But I for one am glad you chose your particular specialty, Dr. Britton." His eyes were gleaming emeralds, filled with insinuation, and as they dropped to the open folds of her robe flames suddenly rose in their depths, like sparks escaping an untended fire.

"How are you feeling?" She drew the edges of her robe back together, forcing her voice into a professional tone.

"Laurel—"

"I do hope you weren't too vigorous on your date," she said swiftly, not willing to accept the way his lush voice embraced her name. "I probably should have warned you to stay away from positions number forty-nine and eighty-seven with that knee....

"After all, McGraw, it may be my job to glue you back together after a game, but any injuries you get on your own time are your responsibility." Laurel knew she'd begun to babble but was helpless to stop.

"Dammit, Laurel, I didn't come over her for a round of verbal sparring."

"Why did you come over?" she asked, honestly curious.

He shrugged. "I don't know."

Nick stared down into the dark chocolate depths of his mug, as if the swirling liquid held some special meaning for him. When he slowly lifted his gaze to her face, his expression was unnervingly solemn.

"I think I wanted to explain about this evening."

"Your date?"

He nodded.

Laurel rose immediately, taking her empty mug to the sink and rinsing it before putting it into the dishwasher. She kept her back to Nick the entire time.

"Don't worry about it, Nick. I never expected anything because of last night. Good heavens, who was it who said 'one swallow doesn't make a summer'?"

"Aristotle." He amazed Laurel by answering her rhetorical question.

She turned around and stared at him, wishing she could understand this man who had more facets to his personality than a well-cut diamond.

"Aristotle," she repeated slowly. Then, gathering her scattered thoughts, she nodded firmly. "Well, just as one swallow doesn't make a summer, one kiss certainly doesn't make a love affair. So don't worry about me misunderstanding, Nick."

He was standing over her in two long strides. "We shared two kisses last night, Laurel. Not one. I'm hurt you could forget so easily."

She was suddenly drowning in the warm green pools of his eyes and Laurel knew Nick could read the answering spark in her own gaze.

"I didn't forget."

Nick reminded himself that while Laurel was attractive and definitely appealing, especially wearing this silky robe that displayed her long slender legs, his telephone directory was filled with women who were just as attractive, just as appealing, and didn't expect anything but a good time.

That was a lie, he admitted inwardly. He knew of no woman as appealing as Laurel Britton. Why hadn't he met her two years ago? Before his perfect life had begun unraveling at the seams.

"I didn't forget, either," he muttered, pulling her against him.

His mouth suddenly ground on hers in a bruising kiss that threatened to take her breath away. Nick's frustration with his situation made him rash; there was none of the tenderness he'd displayed with those experimental kisses of last night. He was all primitive male as he wanted and he took, his burning need spiraling out of control. His tongue stabbed its way between her shocked lips and his mouth crushed hers in an electric, endless demand.

At the first startling impact, a kaleidoscope of swirling colors exploded behind Laurel's eyes, releasing the desire that had been building up for this man all night. Her fingers moved up his arms, digging into his broad shoulders as she clung to his strength. She gave herself up entirely to his raw masculine demands, wanting his superior power, in truth, needing it. Nick's overwhelming physical force and brutal aggression was allowing her to fling aside her rigid mental restraints, meeting him with an equal passion of her own.

Nick groaned his approval as Laurel's tongue slipped between his harsh male lips, sweeping the dark cavern of his mouth, gathering in the moisture from every secret corner. She dragged her fingers through his wheat-blond hair, holding his head in her palms as she deepened the kiss, her own need no gentler than his, her own demands no less desperate.

His arms tightened about her, and as she rose up on her toes, he could feel her warm, pliant female shape fitting itself to him from her breasts to her thighs. He was standing on the very brink of sanity and as he tugged on the sash of the blue satin robe, opening it to allow his palms to skim her body, Nick knew there would be no turning back.

Laurel closed her eyes to the erotic torment of Nick's hands roving her body at will. Reason was scattered to the four winds as she allowed him forbidden intimacies, encouraged him with her breathless cries of pleasure. As Nick's fingers grasped her buttocks, the soft swell of her breasts, the satiny skin of her inner thighs, his touch was everything she'd imagined and more. So much more. His hands were everywhere, leaving a warmth that engulfed her in a cresting tide of desire. When her own fingers began to tear at the buttons of his dress shirt, Nick covered her hand with his own, lifting her wrist to his lips for a brief kiss. His eyes flamed as they burned into hers, holding her gaze as he deftly opened his shirt with one hand. His skin burned with the need for her touch and as Laurel's palms pressed against his chest, Nick sucked in a deep harsh breath.

In a slower, sensual response, his hands traced her slender curves, like conquerors mapping out an exotic, foreign territory. She was so incredibly soft; her skin seemed to flow warmly under his touch, like liquid satin. Nick dragged his mouth from Laurel's, pressing his cheek against the silky strands of her hair, breathing in the lushly fragrant scent of floral shampoo. Her arms wrapped around him and her hands splayed over his back as she arched her body against his in a spiraling feminine need.

He was unable to stifle the groan as he sucked the

air into his lungs on a harsh breath. Laurel suddenly froze.

"You're hurt!" Her wide brown eyes searched his face, seeking the truth there first.

Damn! He shrugged in a dismissing gesture. "Football players are always hurt." His palms shaped her shoulders, encouraging her to forget the untimely interruption. "And just in case you've any questions along those lines, let me assure you all the important parts are in full working order."

But Laurel backed away a few inches, her eyes narrowing. "Don't joke about this, Nick. I probed all around that knee yesterday without you flinching, and it had to have been tender. You've a very high tolerance for pain, so for you to moan like that, something's definitely wrong."

Her fingers began to move over him, their intent more precise, more determined than the graceful fluttering pattern they'd danced on his skin a moment earlier.

"That was merely a moan of passion," he tried, knowing that the mood had been shattered for tonight.

Laurel didn't answer, intent upon her examination. When she pressed against his rib cage, Nick drew in an involuntary breath.

"Lift up your arms," she instructed.

"Not until you answer a question for me."

Her fingers were carefully tracing a line from his side to the center of his chest. Laurel was furious, but certainly not at Nick, and she tried to keep the anger from her voice. But her words came out short and crisp.

"What now, McGraw?"

"Are we finished with the passionate part of this evening?" The sight of her forbidden pearly skin was making concentration difficult. He forced his gaze to a point somewhere beyond Laurel's left shoulder.

She looked up, finding his face an inscrutable mask. "Yes," she acknowledged with a sigh. "It was a bad idea in the first place."

"I don't know, I kind of enjoyed it," he argued, gritting his teeth as her fingers probed deeper into his flesh. "Very much, actually."

"So did I," she admitted. "But we've satisfied as much curiosity as I'm going to allow." Laurel didn't miss Nick's short intake of breath as her fingers hit home.

"Ow!"

"That's what I thought. You've cracked a rib." She shook her head. "You're lucky that's all that happened, the way you were throwing yourself under those linebackers during practice. I thought you weren't going to try to be a hero."

"Believe me, Laurel, I didn't try to get in those guys' way. It certainly isn't my idea of fun being run over by 225 pounds of human mountain."

"I don't understand why they were hitting you like that," she complained. Nick read the distress in her soft brown eyes and wondered how it could affect him so deeply. Everything about Laurel Britton hit like a jolt of lightning from a clear blue sky. Nick wasn't certain he liked the feeling.

"They want to play," he said simply, grimacing as he tried a careless shrug. "If they don't play by Carr's rules, they'll be warming the bench Sunday. It's his way or the highway, that's what he's fond of quoting to the press."

"Sometimes I think you're all crazy." She sighed with heartfelt exasperation. "At least promise me you'll wear your flak jacket Sunday."

He was relieved they weren't going to get into an argument, not being in the mood to explain how important this upcoming game was. How vital this season was. He was Nick McGraw, star quarterback. That's who he'd been for as long as he could remember, and Nick didn't know how to separate the man from the football player, even if he'd wanted to. Which he damn well didn't.

"Cross my heart and hope to die," he pledged, making a corresponding sign over his bare chest. A wicked light danced in his green eyes. "Uh, Laurel, are you sure you're not interested in indulging in a little heavy breathing?"

Her soft, caring gaze hardened. "I hate it when you slip into that automatic seduction routine."

A smile played on his lips. "That's a nope, right?"

"Right."

"Then could you do me a favor, Dr. Britton?"

She eyed him suspiciously. "What kind of favor?"

Nick rubbed his palm over his face, shaking his head with regret. "Could you please tie the sash on that robe? It's awfully hard to behave with temptation so deliciously near."

She glanced down, realizing in her concern for Nick she'd forgotten all about her state of undress. She wrapped the material about herself, yanking the sash tight.

"You should have said something."

He arched an incredulous eyebrow. "Hey, I thought we'd at least determined I'm not a dumb jock. Why should I give up such delectable scenery?"

Her eyes flashed dangerously. "You're incorrigible, McGraw."

"I honestly tried to tell you, Laurel. But Dr. Britton was too busy sadistically poking her lovely fingers into my battered old flesh."

Laurel's anger dissolved as rapidly as it had flared and her brow furrowed with concern. "It's far from old, Nick. And it would be in perfect condition if you'd just quit playing football."

His face turned to stone. "Don't even suggest that," he warned in a cold, remote tone. "Because it isn't going to happen."

He was kidding again. He had to be. "Sure," she shot back flippantly. "You're going to be playing until they carry you off the field at the ripe old age of ninety-nine. And I'll be submitting all your doctor bills to Medicare."

He raked his fingers through his sun-streaked hair and from the way they were trembling with restrained fury, Laurel realized Nick found nothing humorous about the turn their conversation had taken.

"You and Carr should get together and take that act on the road." His tone was harsh as he turned on his heel and marched out the door, slamming it thunderously behind him.

Laurel was left to stare out into the dark, stunned by this newest aspect of Nick McGraw's frustratingly complex personality.

At least the rain had cooled things off, Laurel considered, breathing in the fresh desert air as she drove to the clinic the next morning with the car windows down. Her uplifted spirits plummeted as she reached her office, finding it occupied by two burly workmen.

"Roof leaked last night," one of them explained, pointing to the gaping hole above her desk.

She grimaced at the stack of damp papers on her desk. "Is my office the only one affected?"

"Nope. The private treatment rooms are going to be out of commission for a while, too. The tar paper pulled loose on this part of the building." He shook his head. "Can't trust these flat roofs in the rain," he advised, returning to his work.

Laurel wasn't looking forward to working another day in the fishbowl atmosphere of the common treatment room, under the intense scrutiny of Dr. Adams, but realized pragmatically she had no choice. Stifling a sigh, she went to work.

"Dr. Britton, there's a call for you on line five."

Laurel glanced up sometime later from the pulled hamstring she'd been examining. "Can you get a number and I'll return the call?"

"Sure." The receptionist was back a moment later. "Mr. McGraw says he'll hold."

Laurel didn't miss Tony Lee's smug smile. "All right," she said, picking up the receiver of the wall phone. "Hello."

"I just called to tell you I'll pick Danny up today," Nick began without preamble.

"That's not necessary."

"But I want to."

This was definitely no place for a personal conversation. Tony was displaying unabashed interest as he rummaged through a stack of wrist splints and Laurel could feel Dr. Adams's gray eyes directed at her back.

"Thank you anyway," she replied briskly, "but I'd really prefer you didn't."

"Would it help if I apologized?" Nick asked, his voice deep and beguiling.

"No."

"I am sorry, you know."

"Well, thank you for calling," Laurel said lightly, wanting to end this conversation before it became so personal every interested bystander in the treatment room would know the intimate details of her life.

Nick instantly perceived her intention. "If you hang up, Laurel, you're only going to have to continue this conversation in person. Because I'll be down at the clinic in a half hour."

"You're not on my schedule," she complained.

"Pencil me in as an emergency," he instructed, his firm tone indicating he expected nothing less.

Laurel experienced a momentary stab of concern. "Are you all right? Is it your knee?"

"My knee's fine," he assured her instantly. "It's my ribs. I need them taped before practice."

"That's what the team has trainers for, Nick."

"I'd rather have you do it. See you in a while, Dr. Britton." He hung up the phone.

"That will be fine then, Mr. McGraw," Laurel said into the disconnected telephone, unwilling to let the others know he'd hung up on her. "I'll be expecting you."

"More trouble with that knee?" Tony asked.

"No. He cracked a rib and needs it taped up."

"I thought trainers usually did that," he offered guilelessly.

Laurel shot him a mock glare. "Don't push it, Lee. Or you'll be back on coffee duty."

"Please spare us that unspeakable indignity, Dr. Britton," Dr. Adams murmured as he left the room. "Yours, while definitely not gourmet, is at least drinkable."

Laurel watched him go, then shrugged, unable to tell whether the man had made a joke or not. She didn't know who had ever stated women were the complicated sex; men easily won that title, hands down.

She didn't even need to glance toward the door; the flurry of activity twenty minutes later could only mean one thing. Nick had arrived. Refusing to be part of the crowd of females surrounding him, she leaned against her treatment table, watching as he made his way across the room.

"Like Moses parting the Red Sea," she murmured.

"I'm afraid that reference escapes me," he admitted with a smile.

Laurel shrugged. "I was just observing the way you forged your way through that sea of admirers." She turned her back, pulling out a roll of wide tape. "Sit up and take your shirt off, McGraw."

He didn't move. "Is it that you don't like athletes in general? Or is it me in particular?"

Laurel's back was still to him. "I told you, I like athletes. Professionally," she tacked on with pointed emphasis.

"But not personally."

She turned around, her expression firmly set into one of brisk impatience. "Are you going to take your shirt off so I can tape up that rib? You *are* cutting into my schedule, you know. The least you can do is to be cooperative."

The soft violet shadows under her eyes were mute testimony to the fact she hadn't managed any more sleep last night than he had. Encouraged, Nick held his ground.

"Answer my question first."

"Look, McGraw, I've already spent four long years with one man who wanted to be treated like God. If I was masochistic enough to get involved with another, I'd simply go somewhere they practice self-flagellation."

His green eyes narrowed dangerously, and she was intrigued by the muscle jerking along his thrusting jawline. Before she could utter a word of complaint, his hand was cupping her elbow.

"You're coming with me."

"The hell I am," Laurel retorted in a low harsh whisper, her dark eyes darting around the room to see if they were being observed.

It didn't help to discover she and Nick were the

center of attention. The usually bustling atmosphere had suddenly become as quiet as a tomb, the spectators' attention all directed toward the drama being played out before them.

Nick's gaze followed hers. "Damn." Then, to her utter amazement, his fingers tightened on her arm and he started walking across the floor.

"Nick, let go of me!" It was still a whisper, but easily heard in the swirling silence of the room.

"You can come along with me to your office peacefully, or I'll carry you screaming and kicking over my shoulder," he replied with amazing calm. One look upward into those glittering green eyes assured Laurel he meant every word.

"My office has people working in it," she argued. At his dubious expression, she elaborated. "The roof leaked last night."

"Then we'll go somewhere else," he countered immediately.

"I have other patients."

"This will only take a minute." He continued walking, stopping only momentarily at Tony Lee's treatment table. "Is there someplace private around here?"

Tony nodded in the direction of the hallway. "Third door on your left. It's the doctors' lounge," he stated helpfully.

"Thanks." Nick didn't release Laurel as he continued toward the door.

"Thanks a lot," she ground out over her shoulder at Tony.

He grinned unrepentantly. "My pleasure."

Nick didn't mince words. "All right," he said, the moment they were alone, "you have every right to be angry with me. I behaved like a bastard last night and took out my troubles on you. So, I'm sorry."

"Apology accepted," she said in a tight voice. "Now may I return to my work?"

"This is more important than your work, Laurel!"

She lifted her chin, meeting his furious gaze with a challenging one of her own. "Oh? And what would you do if I marched out onto your precious football field and hauled you off into the showers for a personal conversation?"

A wide smile suddenly lit his face. "Why, I'd offer to wash your back, of course."

"Cute, McGraw. Real cute."

Nick sighed, shaking his head. Laurel tried not to be affected by the way a sun-streaked blond lock fell across his brow, contrasting so vividly with his dark tan.

"I really don't want to fight with you, Laurel. I understand how important your work is. I just want to explain that my behavior last night was due to a personal problem I'm trying to work out. It had nothing to do with you. With us."

"There is no *us*, Nick. Get that through your head right now," she warned.

Even as she said it, Laurel realized it was a lie. She had grown incredibly close to this man in a few short days, but she knew it was only a sexual attraction. He was handsome, famous and actually very nice, when he wasn't coming on like a storm trooper. Any woman would be infatuated. It was nothing more than that, she assured herself—a chemical brain bath.

At this moment, frustrated by Laurel's continued intransigence, Nick could have cheerfully strangled her. "But there is," he argued, hitting one strong fist into his palm. "Number one, we're neighbors—"

"I've read somewhere that the majority of Americans don't know their neighbors' first names," she interrupted.

"Number two, we're friends."

"That's debatable."

He pretended not to hear that one. "And reason number three is that you're going to hurt Danny if you suddenly cut off the practices without a good explanation."

She slumped down into a chair at the table, cupping her chin in her palm as she looked up at him. "If you're honestly concerned about Danny, let's talk about what's going to happen if I let you infiltrate yourself into his life and then you lose interest. That would hurt him a great deal more, Nick."

He had the feeling there was more to Laurel's objection than met the eye, but decided not to press her for the moment. Instead, he sat down next to her, his gaze unbearably serious. "I wouldn't do that, Laurel. You have to believe that."

"I believe you wouldn't mean to; but soon you'd have a lot better ways to spend your time than with a seven-year-old boy. The end result would be the same."

Laurel's expression was intent as she tried to make Nick understand. "Danny's having enough trouble getting over leaving his father. I don't want him to have the same problem with you."

"I'm not going anywhere," he said simply. "Look, we'll stick to being just friends, if that makes you feel any better about the arrangement. And if you want, I'll begin letting Danny down easily, but for now, I think it's helping him adjust to the move."

Laurel sighed a deep, surrendering breath. "All right. But no more late-night visits. It's strictly a good neighbor policy where you and I are concerned, McGraw."

Nick gave her a crooked smile. "You're probably right," he agreed on an answering sigh. "One thing neither of us needs right now is more complications.'' That much was true, but even as Nick agreed he knew he'd never be able to keep his word.

His eyes darkened dangerously. ''But it would've been good, Laurel. Very good.'' He observed her for a long, silent moment. ''Danny can come to practice, then?''

She nodded, unable to force an answer past the lump in her throat.

''I can bring him home,'' Nick offered. ''Save you a trip downtown.''

Laurel asked herself if she could honestly bar Nick McGraw from her house if he showed up at her door. Especially since Danny would undoubtedly ask Nick to stay for dinner. It would be inviting disaster, she decided.

''Don't bother. I'll pick him up at the field.''

''Promise not to get into any brawls with Coach Carr?'' A familiar, dancing light reappeared in his eyes.

Laurel managed a shaky smile. ''I promise to be on my best behavior.''

''Good.'' His answering grin grew a little wider. ''It would play havoc with my tough-guy image if a woman started fighting my battles for me.''

''Your doctor's supposed to watch out for your welfare, Nick,'' she reminded him softly.

''And such a lovely doctor you are, Laurel Britton,'' he murmured, his eyes softening as he gazed down at her thoughtfully. Laurel was certain she'd stopped breathing when he reached out and lightly brushed his knuckles along her cheek. ''Absolutely lovely.'' Then he opened the door, preparing to leave.

''Your rib.'' Laurel belatedly recalled Nick's purpose in coming to the clinic in the first place.

He winked a bright emerald eye. ''Hey, lady— what do you think they have trainers for?''

# 6

LAUREL FELL into a familiar pattern of working at the clinic, then stopping by the Thunderbirds' practice field to pick up Danny. Nick kept his distance, and although it admittedly bothered her, she knew she'd made the right decision.

She'd planned a private party at home to celebrate completing her first week at her new job and had picked up the makings for spaghetti and meatballs—Danny's favorite.

"Look what Nick gave me," he greeted her, waving his prize over his head like a banner as he ran up to her. "They're tickets for Sunday's game. On the fifty-yard line!"

Laurel had known she wouldn't be able to ignore the upcoming game. She'd told herself it was only because she was concerned about Nick's knee. It was a professional interest, nothing more. She'd told herself that over and over again, but at no time had it sounded the least bit convincing, even to her own ears.

She forced a smile. "That's terrific. I hope you thanked him."

As he climbed into the car, Danny gave her a severe look that reminded her uncomfortably of Geoffrey. "Of course I did. What do you think I am, a dope?"

Laurel shook her head. "Certainly not. How could such an intelligent woman as myself have a less than brilliant son?" Then she delicately attempted to minimize the bond that was developing between Nick and her son. "You know, honey, I wouldn't expect Nick to give us tickets to all his home games."

Bright blue eyes observed her questioningly. "Why not? He's my best friend. And I'm taking great care of Rowdy."

He had certainly done that, Laurel admitted. She'd grown used to having the huge animal underfoot. On the first visit she'd locked Circe in the bedroom, but the Siamese's strident complaints had only increased the animosity between the two animals. Finally, she'd given up and to her amazement, after an initial few moments of mistrust, the two had settled into a truce. At times, watching her cat bat playfully at the wide sweeping golden tail, Laurel could almost imagine they'd begun to like each other.

"It's possible he might want to give his tickets to someone else," she suggested carefully. "We don't want to take up too much of Nick's time."

"I don't take up too much of his time. Besides, he likes kids. He's got loads of brothers and sisters."

"Really?" Laurel wasn't particularly surprised. Nick's behavior with Danny had seemed almost too easy, too casual for a single man.

"Yeah. Eight of them."

"Eight?"

Danny nodded. "He's the oldest."

Laurel wondered how her son had discovered this amazing fact. "When did he tell you that?"

He shrugged, looking out the car window, his attention on the palm trees flanking the roadway. "I dunno. We just talk." He turned toward her, looking somewhat guilty. "I guess I was kinda telling him how it got lonely around here sometimes."

Laurel managed to keep her expression nonchalant. "I suppose it does. But you'll be making friends soon and then it'll get better."

"Friends aren't brothers and sisters," he pointed out with the straightforward logic of a seven-year-old. "How come I don't have any brothers or sisters?"

*Because your father was upset enough about me getting pregnant with you,* Laurel thought. "We've discussed this before, Danny," she replied calmly. "Your father and I were both in medical school when you were born. Then he had his internship and his residency, and I went back to school.... We just didn't think we could give enough time to two children."

"I would have helped."

She smiled, reaching over to pat his knee. He was wearing shorts and she smiled at how tanned he'd already become in less than a week. He had skin like Geoffrey's. It wasn't dark, but it tanned easily, despite his reddish hair and freckles. She, on the other hand, could probably live in Phoenix her entire life and still have milky-white skin. Laurel sighed, certain the women Nick dated probably sported tans the color of dark, golden honey. She couldn't compete, even if she wanted to. *Which I don't,* Laurel reminded herself firmly.

She returned to the conversation. "I know you'd be a big help, Danny. But it's a moot point. I'm not married any longer, so you're going to have to settle for Circe and me."

"You could always marry Nick."

"What?"

From the earnest expression on her son's face, Laurel realized Danny had been giving the matter a great deal of thought. He had a logical mind that went directly to the heart of a problem, quickly and incisively. Another thing he had in common with his father. Sometimes she wondered if Danny had inherited any of her attributes.

The idea of Danny's genetic similarity to Geoffrey

caused an all-too-familiar little spiral of fear to crawl up Laurel's spine. *I won't think about that,* she vowed. *Not tonight. In fact, if the phone rings, I won't even answer it.*

Danny's voice broke into her troubled thoughts. "It's simple, mom," he explained patiently, as if instructing a rather dense kindergartner. "Look, you like kids, right?"

"I like you."

"And Nick likes kids. But neither one of you are married. So if you married each other, your problems would be solved." He nodded, pleased with his reasoning. "You'd have a husband, I'd have a live-in dad, Nick would have a son and then I could have some brothers and sisters."

Then he added what he obviously considered the clincher. "And think of the money you'd both save, only needing one house. We could sell ours and move in with Nick."

"I like our house, Danny," Laurel pointed out. "I thought you did, too."

He rushed in to reassure her. "Hey, it's a great house, mom. But it has stairs."

"May I point out that was one of the things you requested?" she inquired dryly, remembering how long fulfilling that particular request had taken, especially when combined with a pool, walking distance to a good school and a tree in the backyard big enough for a tree house. She'd found everything but the tree. "I seem to recall something about Circe being able to chase her ball down them."

"Yeah, well, that was okay just for us. But stairs would be hard on Nick's bad knee," he pointed out. "I think we should move into his house, instead."

Laurel shook her head. "Danny," she said with a certain amount of alarm, "you haven't discussed this idea with Nick, have you?"

"Not yet," he admitted. "I wanted him to get used to the idea of having me around first."

"Don't," she warned.

"But, mom—"

Laurel's expression was firm as she pulled the car into the driveway. She turned off the engine and took the keys from the ignition. Resting her forearms on top of the steering wheel for a moment, she lowered her forehead to them, garnering strength.

Then giving Danny her sternest look, she said, "If you so much as mention a word of this conversation to Nick, Daniel Patrick Britton, today will be the last practice you ever attend. Is that clear?"

He paled visibly, his freckles darker for the contrast. "Okay, mom," he agreed in a small voice. "It was just an idea."

"Not one word," she repeated, wagging her finger.

He made the gesture he'd learned last year in school, zipping his mouth, locking it and throwing away the key.

Laurel managed a laugh. "That's better. Now, help me carry in the groceries. We're having your favorite dinner."

"Pasghetti?"

"With hot fudge sundaes for dessert."

Danny hurried to help, the subject mercifully dropped. But Laurel knew her son well. He had a habit of worrying a problem to death, if it interested him. She had the uneasy feeling she hadn't heard the last on this particular matter.

LAUREL HAD NEVER BEEN to a professional football game and was stunned at the noise level the crowd made in the bowl-shaped stadium. Danny's hand trembled with excitement as she held it on the way to their seats, but as soon as the team came onto the field, he tugged free. He didn't want Nick to think of him as a child, she realized, watching him straighten to attention. She felt like assuring her son that Nick would be far too busy to spare even a glance in their direction, when Danny started jumping up and down, waving his red-and-gold pennant wildly.

"There he is, mom! Nick! Hey, Nick!"

His high, young voice was drowned out by the volume of the crowd, but to Laurel's amazement, Nick turned, looking directly at them. He grinned—a broad, marvelously attractive smile—and waved his helmet in greeting. For a brief moment his gaze locked with Laurel's and the pleasure in his green eyes at seeing her made her heart turn a series of out-of-control somersaults. Then he lifted his hand, his fingers spread in a V sign, before turning his attention back to the coaches.

"He saw us!"

Laurel nodded. "He certainly did. Now stop waving that thing around before you put someone's eye out." Her voice was firm but the smile on her face belied her tone, and Danny grinned, shoving the pennant under his seat, his enthusiasm not in the least bit dampened.

The game got off to a less than impressive start as the opposing Raiders displayed a brutal ground offense, marching continuously through the Thunderbirds' defensive line for a hard-fought touchdown. Laurel's eyes were on Nick as he paced the sidelines in obvious frustration. A conversion put the Raiders ahead by seven, and as the offensive team took to the field, there were a few scattered shouts for Morgan to go in as quarterback.

Nick caught the snap and went back for a pass, but it was blocked by the Raiders' defensive end. The calls for Morgan increased. A second pass was blocked the same way, this time sent back at Nick as if he'd thrown it into a brick wall. The fans were building up steam, the atmosphere reminding Laurel of the Christians and the lions. She decided if an opinion poll was taken for Nick's survival chances, over half the people in the stadium would put thumbs down.

She saw him shout something at the player who'd blocked the shots, watched that player shout something back, but the roar of the crowd made it impossible to know what had been said.

"Mom!" Danny objected, his eyes wide as he stared at the red-faced fans, all on their feet, shouting for Carr to pull Nick from the game.

"Ignore them, Danny. Nick'll do just fine." She only wished her voice held more conviction.

As they lined up for the third down, Laurel crossed her fingers behind her back, resting her other hand on her son's shoulder. Nick dropped back to pass, scanned the field for a fraction of a second, then tucked the ball and galloped away for the necessary ten yards.

All objections melted away as the fans roared their approval. When three plays later the Thunderbirds were on the scoreboard, opposition to Nick seemed to have become ancient history. After that less than spectacular start the Thunderbirds' defense shut down the Raiders' running attack, and Laurel was relieved as Nick stuck to a passing game the remainder of the afternoon. When the game ended, Nick and his Thunderbirds had won, 31–7.

If Danny was ecstatic, Laurel was no less so, her voice hoarse, her throat sore from screaming. She felt like a child herself as they jumped up and down, hugging each other wildly. When Nick looked up at where they were celebrating, she waved Danny's banner, her smile reaching from ear to ear.

It took the rest of the evening to get Danny calmed

down enough to go to sleep. He'd begged to go over and congratulate Nick, but judging by the continuous stream of sports cars roaring up to the house next door, Laurel decided it was certainly no place for an idealistic young boy. Assuring her son he'd see Nick tomorrow, she put him to bed, smiling as he fell promptly asleep, running down abruptly like a spring-wound clock.

She sat alone out by the pool, listening to the music and the cacophonous sounds from the wild party going on next door. No wonder the real estate agent had neglected to mention Nick McGraw was her neighbor. If it was going to be like this every Sunday night, she'd be a wreck on Monday mornings. Laurel glared in the direction of the gate in the shared wall, wishing she had the nerve to march over there right now and tell him to quiet things down. Tomorrow, she vowed, tomorrow she'd confront him after practice and insist he behave with more consideration for his neighbors.

She'd just gone in to pour herself another cup of coffee when the phone rang.

"Hello?"

"Laurel?" She wasn't surprised he couldn't hear her. The music in the background was deafening.

"Nick? Turn down the music."

"What?"

"I said, turn down the music!" she shouted.

"I still can't hear you, Laurel. Can you hear me?"

"Barely," she shouted a little louder, wondering why she was even trying. She should just hang up. "What do you want?"

"I need you over here, Laurel," he yelled. A female giggle came over the wires.

"It sounds like you're doing just fine without me, McGraw," she said, furious he had the nerve to invite her to his damn party this late. Not that she would have gone if he'd suggested it earlier. She slammed the receiver down, deciding he could undoubtedly hear that well enough.

Seconds later her phone rang again. "Look, not that anyone could get any sleep around here, but I'd like to try. So knock it off," she shouted.

There was dead silence on the other end. "I really do need you, Laurel," he said finally. She could still hear the party noise in his backyard and wondered where he'd gone that it was suddenly so quiet.

"Where are you?"

"In my bedroom. Alone."

"That shouldn't prove an unsolvable problem. Just open the door and you'll have to fight the women away with a stick."

"I don't know if I can make it to the door."

His low, pained tone caused ice water to run through her veins. "Is it your knee?" she whispered, clutching the receiver with suddenly moist hands.

"That's right. My knee." She heard a muffled groan. "I really do need you, Laurel."

"Give me two minutes to dress and I'll be right there." Laurel hung up the phone, flinging off her robe and nightgown as she ran up the stairs to her bedroom. She pulled a pair of jeans and a T-shirt out of her closet, throwing them on her body, not taking time for anything else. Soon she was through the gate and pushing her way through the throng, desperate to get to him.

"Are you the doc?" A huge man with a neck the circumference of a tree trunk came up to her, eyeing her bag.

"That's right. I'm Dr. Britton."

"Tom Shaw," he introduced himself, sticking out an enormous hand. "I'm the one who's supposed to keep Nick from getting that pretty face bashed in.... He's in the house. I'll show you the way," he offered.

"Is he hurt badly?" she asked as he led her down a long hallway.

Tom answered with an enigmatic smile. "I think he'll be fine now." He opened the door. "Good luck, Nick. I think you're going to need it," he called before making a hasty retreat.

Nick was seated on the end of a wide bed, his forearms on his thighs, his hands clasped loosely together between his knees. Laurel rushed to kneel beside him.

"Can you take those jeans off by yourself, or do you need some help?"

He slowly lifted his head, his green eyes brightening considerably. "Now that is, without a doubt, the most inviting offer I've had all evening."

Laurel studied Nick suspiciously, not seeing the expected shadowing of pain in his eyes. "Your knee," she reminded him.

He gave her a tentative smile. "My knee is fine, Laurel."

She was on her feet instantly. "You lied to me, Nick McGraw! You said you needed me."

"I didn't lie. I do need you." He lifted his palms in a helpless gesture. "I'll admit I stretched the truth about my leg a little in order to get you over here. I didn't think you'd come otherwise." He looked at her curiously. "Would you have?"

As his gaze settled disconcertingly on her breasts, Laurel remembered she'd neglected to put on a bra. She crossed her arms over her chest.

"Of course not. I'm not into orgies."

He sighed, raking his fingers through his hair as he rose to stand over her. "It's only a party."

Laurel turned away, preparing to leave. "Sure, try telling that to the vice squad when they raid the place. Do you usually have an entire line of nearly naked cheerleaders dancing on your kitchen counter?"

"Laurel..."

She stopped, unable to walk away from the request in his low voice. But she refused to turn around, knowing she'd never survive the expression he was probably directing her way.

"What is it?"

"I'm lonely, Laurel. That's why I called you."

"Lonely?" She managed a brittle laugh. "Take a look out there, Nick," she advised, waving her hand in the direction of his backyard. "Between the house and the yard there must be two hundred people roaming around this place. Two hundred very noisy people," she tacked on pointedly.

He came up behind her. Although he hadn't yet touched her, Laurel could feel the heat of his body unnervingly near her back. He bent his head, his words a mint-sprigged summer breeze in her ear.

"Haven't you ever been lonely in the middle of a crowd?" he asked softly.

Of course she had. Innumerable times when she'd attended parties with Geoffrey. But that had never seemed so unusual. She'd been lonely at home with her ex-husband, too.

"That's the worst kind of lonely, Laurel." He pressed his case. "Because you realize that you need something more than mere bodies. You need one special person to make everything all right again."

Even as he uttered the seductive words, Nick realized they were true. Unwilling to try to decode why these atypical emotions kept surfacing whenever he was around Laurel, he forced his mind to focus on the obvious. Like the soft scent of wild flowers wafting from her skin. The glossy sheen of her nut-dark hair. And the way her body was trembling of its own volition. Nick knew she was afraid, just as he knew every nerve in her body mirrored his own overwhelming need.

"I'm not that person," she protested in a whisper, wrapping her arms about herself in an unconsciously protective gesture. *Don't listen to this*, she instructed her mind. But she was fast discovering a rosy cloud had settled over her brain and she was left with only her feelings.

"Yes, you are. And I know I'm a rat to take advantage of you like this, but I managed to win a very important game today. A game that meant a lot more to me than the final score would indicate. I want to share that victory with one very special person."

He hesitated, his hands going lightly around her waist as he drew her back against him. "I want... no, I need to share these feelings with you, lovely Laurel. Please don't turn me down."

Oh dear Lord, how could she refuse a request like that? "I can't stay here, Nick," she said slowly, turning in his arms to look up at him. "Danny's asleep alone. I only left him because I thought it was an emergency."

Their eyes held and there was a moment of heat as Nick appeared on the brink of kissing her. But he refrained, shaking his head with a soft sigh.

"It *was* an emergency. I had to see you, Laurel. I had to hold you like this. I had to feel how perfectly you fit into my arms."

"Nick—"

"We'll go over to your house," he said simply. "Then Danny won't be alone."

Laurel knew she was playing with a fire that was on the verge of blazing wildly out of control. But it felt so good to have Nick's arms around her, it felt so wonderfully right to have him looking at her, his green eyes smoldering with undisguised desire.

She fought for a lifeline of sanity, forcing herself

to throw away the blinders and face his reputation straight on. "I don't know how you usually celebrate a victory, Nick. But as marvelous as today's was, it isn't going to end with you in my bed."

He nodded. "Fair enough." He ran his hand down her side, tracing her slender curves. "I'm not going to lie and say I don't want to make love to you, Laurel. But I'm willing to respect your ground rules. If all we do is talk, that'll be okay, too."

Her soft brown eyes mirrored her vacillation. "Promise?"

"Scout's honor."

That earned a light laugh. "I find it hard to believe the host of that party out there was ever a Boy Scout."

"Eagle Scout. My dad was scoutmaster, actually."

For some odd reason, it was a surprise to think of Nick with a family. Laurel decided perhaps if they got to know each other better, grew more comfortable with each other, this constant attraction would fade. She seriously doubted that, but she wanted to come up with some excuse for allowing Nick to return to her house with her.

"How can you leave your own party?"

He shrugged. "Don't worry about it. No one will notice I'm gone except Tom, and he'll figure out where I am easily enough."

Laurel wondered what kind of friends these were that they were supposed to be here celebrating Nick's victory and wouldn't even care enough to notice he'd disappeared. She and Nick McGraw obviously moved in different circles. They were light-years apart and no amount of sexual chemistry was ever going to change that.

"Just for a while," she warned.

He smiled, brushing a kiss as light as a snowflake

against her lips. "Just for a while," he agreed. "Thank you, Laurel."

She gave a brief nod, finding his grave note of sincere appreciation did nothing to instill calm.

# 7

"AH, PEACE." Nick sighed happily as he sank down onto Laurel's living-room sofa. He linked his fingers behind his head, resting it against the muted striped material as he closed his eyes.

"If peace and quiet were what you were seeking tonight, you've got an awfully funny way of showing it," Laurel pointed out.

He opened one eye. "You sure know how to get to the heart of the matter, don't you, Dr. Britton?"

Then he surprised her by suddenly sitting up straight and looking at her with a certain amount of censure. "Don't you ever have any self-doubts? Or are you so confident about your abilities you can't imagine being like the rest of us poor slobs?"

Laurel stared down at him, wondering where he'd gotten that mistaken impression. Could she possibly come off so cold, so unfeeling? Self-doubts? Good Lord, her life was filled with them. But they were too personal, went too deep and hurt too painfully to share them with anyone. Especially Nick, who had demonstrated all too clearly that depth wasn't what he looked for in a woman.

He gave a sigh, but this time it lacked the pleased note it had a moment earlier. "Do you have anything to drink around here?"

"I've got some coffee," she offered. "Or if you'd like something a little stronger, I think there's a bottle of brandy that managed to arrive down here unbroken."

"Brandy would be terrific," he agreed. "The adrenaline from the game is starting to wear off and I think I need an analgesic.''

She gave him a concerned look. "Is your knee hurting?''

Nick smiled, shaking his head. "Honey, my entire body feels like it's been run over by a steamroller."

Laurel opened her mouth to tell him that perhaps he should consider quitting, if this was all the reward he received. But she held her tongue, knowing that when they had that conversation, she'd stand a better chance of making Nick listen to reason when he wasn't so tired. Lines she'd never noticed before were etched into his tanned face and she experienced an inexplicable urge to reach out and stroke them away with her fingertips.

"I'll get the brandy,'' she told him instead.

He nodded, closing his eyes once more as he leaned his head against the back of the sofa. Sweet. Despite her often irritatingly professional demeanor, the woman was undeniably sweet. And soft. God, how incredibly soft. As he fantasized holding Laurel in his arms, making love to her with uninhibited abandon, Nick drifted off into oblivion.

"Here you are.''

His eyes flew open as Laurel sat down beside him and she had the feeling he'd been asleep. "You should be in bed,'' she scolded.

The heat was still surging through his veins. "I agree. *We* should be in bed.''

Laurel fought the response his deeply crooned suggestion created deep within her. "You promised, Nick,'' she reminded him firmly.

Give it time, he warned himself. Just a little more time. Her pupils were wide and dark, her brown eyes giving away her deepest secrets as they gleamed with an alien heat. Nick managed a casual, yet admittedly regretful tone.

"So I did, Laurel. So I did." He nodded reluctantly, taking the glass from her hand. "Thank you."

As he lifted the glass to his lips, Laurel received a definite jolt. Did everything about this man have to affect her so erotically? It was absolute folly to be sitting here, so close to him, the lights low, the stillness of her home, in direct contrast to the bedlam next door, making the mood seem all the more intimate.

As the bracing liquor cleared his mind, Nick tried to remind himself he was a civilized man. He could not give in to instinct and ravish Laurel right there and then. He damned that pledge he'd made, although he knew that if he hadn't, she wouldn't have allowed him to be sitting there at the moment. He wanted her—Lord, how he wanted her—more than he'd ever wanted a woman in his life. He tried to tell himself it was only to cap off the day in style, to achieve a victory on all fronts, but something in that explanation rang false.

She'd been driving him crazy since the beginning, infiltrating his thoughts, disturbing his sleep. He saw her in his mind's eye when he was supposed to be concentrating on plays—she appeared to him in a myriad of ways and images, constantly changing, like the facets of a child's kaleidoscope. Who the hell was the lovely Dr. Laurel Britton, he wondered. And what was she doing to his mind? To his life?

"I enjoyed the game today," she murmured into the deep silence, running her fingernail along the rim of her glass.

"I'm glad. I'm also glad you came."

"I couldn't very well let Danny down," she replied, struggling to school her voice to a calm nonchalance.

How could she tell him that it would have been impossible to stay away from the game because she'd already discovered it was an impossibility to stay away from him?

"Of course not," he agreed brusquely. "We have to let him down gently."

So that's all it was. A maternal duty. The very idea made Nick feel like a fool for the rush of pleasure he'd experienced when he'd seen her in the stands.

"That's the kindest way."

"I suppose you know best."

"I do." Her firm expression included more than her decision about her son's relationship with Nick McGraw. Even more important was the fact that she was not going to become involved with the man.

*Sure,* taunted the little voice of reason deep inside her. *That's why you're sitting inches apart in a dimly lit room, sipping brandy with him.*

Nick could no longer be this near Laurel without touching her; every atom in his body was screaming with anticipation. Feeling like a teenager on his first date, he carefully slid his arm around her shoulders. He didn't miss her quick little intake of breath as his fingers curved lightly about her upper arm, but she didn't protest.

"What did you yell at that player today?" she asked blankly, trying to concentrate on something—any-thing—besides the warmth of his touch on her bare skin.

He took a drink, eyeing her curiously. "Which one?"

"The big one," she managed to answer as his long fingers created havoc with their gentle strokes.

That earned a smile. "Laurel, football players are all big. Could you be a little more specific?"

God, he agonized, her skin was so fragrant, so silky. How could she expect him to keep his mind on football? For the first time in his life, Nick wished he'd never heard of the game.

As the dangerous hand moved down her arm, Laurel felt as if he'd taken a sparkler to her skin. She drew in a deep breath, attempting to focus on this conversation.

"The one who blocked your first two passes."

Nick watched her breasts rise and fall with her breathing under the scant covering of blue cotton and had to grip the stem of his glass to keep his other hand from reaching out and touching her.

His eyes flamed with emerald fire as their gazes met and held. "Oh, him. I told him to stay down."

"Oh," she whispered, engulfed by the warmth directed her way. "But I saw him yell back. What did he say?"

"You have the loveliest mouth, Laurel. It reminds me of an old-fashioned Gibson girl. What do they call it, a Cupid's bow?"

"Something like that," she stammered softly. "What did he say?"

"It just begs to be kissed." His head moved a little closer, his fingers tightening perceptibly on her arm.

"I don't believe he said that," she argued, entranced as his blond head drew nearer. Her lips parted slightly in anticipation as he took her glass from her hand and laid it down with his onto the table in front of them with a slow, deliberate motion. At no time did his eyes leave her mouth.

"You're right. That's not what he said. He warned me that the next one would be an interception. So I surprised the hell out of everyone who thought I couldn't move with this knee and ran the play instead.... Would I be breaking the rules if I kissed you?"

"Yes." It was a not very assertive whisper.

"Then you're going to be forced to call a penalty, sweetheart. Because I'm about to break the rules."

Nick groaned a gentle oath and with that his lips

finally bridged the distance, his satisfied sigh filling her mouth. There was no hint of urgency in his manner; it was as if they both surpassed the ordinary realm of time and space as he tasted of Laurel's sweet lips at his leisure.

How amazing that this man who earned his living in such a brutal fashion could be so gentle, so tender, she thought through the rosy fog clouding her mind. His lips were plucking gently at hers, teasing, coaxing, warming her skin with heat that spread through her body in escalating waves.

Laurel told herself this was madness, insanity. The Nick McGraw who had led his team to victory this afternoon had undoubtedly celebrated this way after winning games since high school. By allowing this behavior, she was permitting herself to be nothing but a long-established tradition. A reward for a game well played. Even as she told herself that, the persuasive, wonderful kiss was sending a delicious whisper of pleasure up and down the delicate bones of her spine. Soon, she promised her practical self. Soon she would end this glorious embrace. But, dear Lord, how she wanted it to go on for just a little longer.

The tip of his tongue brushed along the full upper curve of her lip, stroking with little intoxicating movements, bringing every inch of the soft pink flesh to tingling awareness. When his teeth captured the thrusting curve of her lower lip, Laurel tried to remember that what was sheer ecstasy for her was only a victory ritual for Nick.

"Nick, please," she whispered against his lips.

His tongue soothed where his teeth had darkened her skin. "Please yes?" he inquired on a husky, uneven note. "Or please no?"

Unable to answer, Laurel closed her eyes, as well as her mind to the tormenting voice of reason as his tongue insinuated itself between her ravished lips, flicking like a finger of flame against the sensitized skin within.

Their bodies pressed together as their mouths met in desperate hunger. Laurel was shocked by the extent of her passion — her skin came alive wherever his roaming hand touched, the blood beneath infused with a thick warmth like heated honey. Her lips moved under his, murmuring inarticulate words that caused Nick's own passion to escalate to a point just short of explosion.

He felt her shudder as his hands slipped under the cotton T-shirt to cup her breasts. She felt so good, so right. Her firm breasts swelled at his touch, her nipples tightening as his palms teased their sensitive nerve endings.

It suddenly flashed through Nick's mind that today he'd proved to everyone that they'd written Nick McGraw's obituary prematurely. There'd been no sign of his injury when he surprised the defensive linemen and ran for that first down. The fans had dropped their objections, lining up behind him once again because they could recognize a winner. He had his life back on track. Everything was as it once was, as it should be, including a beautiful willing woman to make his victory taste even sweeter.

Even as he thought all that, Nick realized his hands were shaking. He was in danger of losing control, which made no sense to his beleaguered mind. He'd had every intention of ending up this evening in Laurel's bed, yet he was stunned by the fact that merely kissing her, simply touching her, was driving him to the ragged edge of sanity.

Nick McGraw made love as he played football — with a practiced skill that made every movement seem inordinately natural. Yet as his fingers fumbled desperately with the zipper on Laurel's jeans, the reason why this physical act, which he had performed so many times before in his lifetime, should suddenly seem so new, so different, eluded his understanding. Before he could dwell on that thought any further, Laurel caught his searching hand.

"Nick, I can't." Part of her was crying out for Nick's exquisite lovemaking. But something equally as strong counseled caution. Laurel had no idea what was happening, but instinct told her they were plunging into something far more entangling than a casual affair. And it was all happening too fast.

"Of course you can." His mouth swallowed her weak protest as his teasing touch created havoc within every fiber of her being. "You can't deny you want me as badly as I want you."

Her palms framed his face; her smoky dark eyes spoke volumes. "Of course I want you," she admitted on a soft sigh. "But we can't always have everything we want."

Nick was appalled by the flash of desperation that seared through him as Laurel began to straighten her clothing, covering up that lustrous creamy skin.

"We can damn well try."

"We can try a little patience, too," she argued, moving away to the other end of the couch.

Laurel knew her behavior could easily be considered irrational and dangerous. She was a grown woman, she knew better than to allow things to get out of control like this. Nick was so much stronger than she, and at the moment his blistering expression was anything but encouraging. If he chose to finish what they'd both begun, Laurel knew she'd be powerless to stop him.

Laurel's obvious trepidation only served to irritate Nick further. While he hated to let her go, he'd never used force on a woman yet and he wasn't about to begin with this one.

"Patience is an overrated virtue... Dammit, Laurel, this is ridiculous! I want you. You want me. We're both adults, so what is the matter?"

Laurel desperately wished she knew. "I never meant for this to happen," she said softly. "Not tonight."

"I did," he admitted, rising from the couch in an abrupt movement. He retrieved his glass of brandy, downing the amber liquid in long, thirsty swallows.

"But you promised," she reminded him softly.

He shrugged, trying for a nonchalant attitude. "I lied."

"Oh."

Laurel reached out with trembling hands, picking up her own glass from the table. She eyed him thoughtfully as she sipped the comforting brandy, taking in his rigid stance. Every muscle in the man's body looked horribly tense.

"You do that very well," she murmured finally.

"Which are you talking about? Making love? Or lying?"

"Both, I suppose."

He turned abruptly, walking over to the desk where she'd left the bottle of brandy. "I've had a lot of practice," he said, refilling his glass. He turned back to her, his green eyes glittering masculine warning. "I'm not giving up, you know."

She met his frank gaze with assumed tranquillity, but an inward tremor. "Hasn't a woman ever turned you down, McGraw?"

He leaned his hips against the desk, crossing his legs at the ankles. "What do you think?"

"I think this just may be a first for the infamous star quarterback."

He shook his head. "You've got it all wrong, Laurel. All you've done tonight is postpone the inevitable."

"With delusions of grandeur like that, I think you need a psychiatrist a lot more than you do a sports doctor," she shot back.

Nick enjoyed watching the spark of fury darken her eyes. God, she was a passionate woman! Making love to her was going to be like trying to tame an erupting volcano.

"Wrong." He grinned maddeningly. "I know one particular sports doctor I need a great deal." He came toward her slowly, his desirous gaze riveted to her face. Their eyes warred for a long, silent moment. Hers were dark and stormy, his glittered with dangerous, masculine purpose.

"Someone really ought to tell you that you're not irresistible," she said in a low voice.

Nick maintained his bland smile. "Don't you find me even moderately irresistible?"

"Hardly." Laurel waited irrationally for the bolt of lightning to strike her for telling such an outrageous lie.

Her haughty tone caused his own temper to flare, but Nick fought to control it. He did, however, give in to a primitive instinct as he pulled her abruptly off the couch and into his arms.

"Prove it."

She tried to jerk away, but his palm cupped the back of her head. "Nick," she protested, her palms pressing against his shirt.

"Prove it," he repeated once again, his fingers tightening in her hair.

Laurel read the anger in his eyes and fought against the thrill of excitement created by his hard, tense body pressed so intimately against hers. Nick felt her slight tremor, and guided by some inner compulsion, he found his world centered for a dangerous, suspended time on this one woman. As they stared at each other, both Nick and Laurel were overwhelmingly shaken. But neither wanted to be the one to admit it.

Nick spoke first. "Next time you won't say no."

"There won't be a next time," she protested softly.

He traced the bow-shaped curve of her mouth with his fingertip. "Oh yes, lovely Laurel, there will definitely be a next time, as well as several after that. I fully intend to make love to you every time those ridiculously seductive lips get within kissing distance." Then, he added silently, having satisfied his curiosity and desire he could get on with rebuilding his life.

He stepped back, eyeing her thoughtfully. "Later," he said, before turning to walk back to his own house and a party that had been a lousy idea to begin with.

Laurel's discerning eyes had not missed his pronounced limp. The physician in her surfaced coming to the rescue of the bewildered woman.

"Would you like that massage I promised you the other night?" she inquired calmly.

Nick looked back over his shoulder, his answering expression incredulous. "Are you serious?"

"Absolutely."

His gaze narrowed. "What kind of massage are we talking about here?"

Laurel had to smile at that. "Don't worry, Mc-Graw, I'm not going to attack you. We've got Dr. Britton back now, and she's the take-charge lady, remember?"

Nick did not mention that he'd been having trouble with that one, too. In fact, he hadn't found one aspect of this woman that didn't intrigue him, make him want to know her better.

"Well?" She was waiting for his answer.

Nick weighed his options. There were any number of beautiful, willing women next door. The night wouldn't have to be a total loss. He frowned as he realized he only wanted Laurel. He didn't want to dilute her taste, diminish the feel of her firm, slender curves with any other companion.

Damn her, he considered with a fresh burst of irritation. She'd infiltrated his system like a drug and as much as he wanted to walk away, he found that he couldn't.

"I think maybe I would like that massage," he answered finally. "After all these years I thought I was well acquainted with every bone in my body. But I discovered a few new ones today."

"I'll get the lotion." She turned away.

"Laurel?"

"Yes, Nick?"

"Are you sure?"

She met his questioning gaze with a level one of her own. "Don't worry, I've yet to rape one of my patients." Her tone was dry and Nick didn't know whether to be irritated or impressed by the way she appeared to have recovered her composure. "You're safe enough."

She escaped the room and as Nick stripped to his shorts he realized Laurel couldn't begin to understand how false a statement that was. He was fast discovering her to be the most dangerous woman he'd ever met.

Laurel leaned against the sink as she splashed cold water over her face, gathering up her scattered senses. Then she tried a variety of expressions in the bathroom mirror until she found one to her liking. There. That looked far more self-confident than she felt.

"My God," she breathed softly as she returned. "You look absolutely terrible."

"Now I know why you're not worried about a near-naked man lying on your couch. A couple more of those ego boosters and I wouldn't be able to do anything, anyway," he grumbled.

Laurel eyed the darkening bruises with deep concern. "This isn't funny; you look like a side of beef."

He glanced down indifferently at his body. "Hey, they'll fade. They always do."

She reached up, tracing the scar that extended outward from his top lip. "Always?" she inquired, arching an argumentative brow.

"Usually. That's just a reminder of what happens when you don't move fast enough to avoid a blitz."

Her worried gaze dropped to his knee. "You don't have that much mobility these days," she argued. "How are you going to avoid those blitzes the rest of the season?"

He shrugged, disliking this subject intensely. "One game at a time, I suppose. The same way I always have."

Laurel spread a towel out on the couch, motioning for him to lie down. "I see. And after the season's over?"

Nick expelled a deep sigh of relief as he stretched out on his stomach, his hands under his chin. "Then I spend the summer working out. Building up the knee some more."

"If it isn't completely destroyed," she muttered under her breath, rubbing some lotion between her hands.

"I didn't quite catch that," he invited.

As Laurel's palms spread over his broad back, she could feel the tension in every muscle. Nick was sore, tired and had ridden an emotional roller coaster all day. This was definitely not the time to bring it up.

"And after the summer?" she forced herself to ask casually.

"Then there's next season," he stated simply.

"I see. And you plan to play next season?"

He looked up over his shoulder at her. "Of course."

"Of course," she repeated softly, having suspected his answer before she'd asked the question. Laurel moved her palms in long, flowing strokes over his back.

"You have nice hands," he murmured, his mind beginning to float comfortably.

"Thank you. And you have very tense muscles."

"That's the name of the game."

"If you're going to be football's old man, McGraw, you're going to have to learn to take better care of your body."

"Hey," he complained as she began kneading the swollen muscle tissue. "I'm in pretty good shape. Better than some of the rookies. I'll have you know, the opening day of training camp I had a 3.25 body-fat ratio. Lowest on the team."

Laurel had no doubt. He was all lean muscle and strong sinew. But he was not a machine. She wondered sadly when he'd realize that fact for himself.

"You should have had this massage hours ago, instead of letting your muscles swell up like this," she scolded, wringing out his tense muscles with a kneading, rolling motion.

"Ah, but I couldn't find anyone at the party who had such great hands."

Laurel couldn't help herself. She pinched him. Hard.

"Ow!"

"Excuse me," she said sweetly. "Speaking of that party, is it going to be a weekly occurrence? I'd like to book Danny's and my hotel room in advance next time."

"Would you believe that's the last one of the year?"

Laurel's fingertips were moving in a deep, slow circular movement, as she sought to break up the muscle knots constricting Nick's blood vessels. "Really?"

He turned his head, looking up at her, his expression serious. "Really. I've always hated them, which is why I quit going to them years ago. Until..." His voice dropped off and Laurel felt his shrug under her fingertips.

"Until your knee injury," she guessed correctly.

He nodded. "It was as if I started acting like a rookie again, then I could play like one." He shot her a warning glance. "Don't you dare laugh. I've spent the past year of my life going crazy."

"I can understand that." Laurel began a vibrating massage along both sides of his spine, encouraging relaxation. "It must have been a shock to have to face a premature end to your career. I can see how regression would be a likely stage."

"Now you sound just like a doctor," he complained.

"I *am* a doctor," she shot back. "And if you want to keep playing, McGraw, you'd better begin treating this body with more respect. I'm prescribing a daily massage and expect your trainer to do it after each practice."

"I don't like his as well as yours," Nick grumbled. "He does all that hitting with the side of his hand. Not to mention his fist. I think the man's a closet sadist."

"Hey, we're getting to that part next," she warned. "Look, Nick—" Laurel's voice turned deadly serious "—this is important. Especially with the practices Carr is giving you. You must feel the difference to your body."

He could definitely feel the change Laurel's wonderful touch was having on him. Not wanting to give up the pleasure, he refrained from the seductive answer that came to mind.

"I know I hurt like hell from all those live hits during practice."

Laurel fought down her temper at the reminder of the Thunderbird coach's obvious strategy to force Nick off the team. "It's more than that. With all the sustained activity you're putting in during practice, you're forcing your blood vessels into a restricted state."

She sought to come up with an example. "Have you ever seen pictures of the New York marathon?"

"I think so," he muttered sleepily. Laurel smiled as she realized the massage was beginning to take.

"Can you recall the runners on the Verrazano-Narrows Bridge?"

"The one where they're all crowded together from one end of it to the other?"

Laurel nodded. "That's it. Think of that bridge as your blood vessels after practice. The millions of blood cells carrying nutrients and waste are all jammed together, and the intake of oxygen and removal of lactic acid become insufficient for the needs of your muscles. So their ability to contract or relax deteriorates. The muscles tighten, your coordination and power diminishes and bang—you're just asking for an injury. I want you to promise you'll have a massage every day, at least during the season."

"I promise, Doc," he agreed.

Laurel smiled, pleased with herself for getting her point across. As a long-distance runner herself, she knew massage could even have a curative effect. She considered it vital to good training, and with the way Nick had accepted her medical advice so easily, she wondered if she might not convince him to see the light and quit altogether, before he was critically injured.

Then he proved once again that he was one step

ahead of her. "I suppose, as my physician, you'd like me most likely to come to you for my daily treatment."

"I already suggested the team trainer," she reminded him, finishing up with a variety of light percussion movements up and down his back.

"I want you."

"Even a famous football star doesn't get everything he wants in life, Nick. It's probably time you learned that little lesson." She increased the strength of her touch considerably.

"Hey, take it easy. Now you're starting to feel like Louie," he complained as her hands tapped vigorously against his back. Then he returned his attention to their argument. "If you refuse to treat me, Laurel, I'll complain to the A.M.A. and they'll take away your license," he warned.

"That's ridiculous," she snapped.

"Really? Haven't you ever heard of the Hippocratic oath? I think you're stuck with me, Dr. Britton."

As Laurel opened her mouth to issue a scathing comment, she realized Nick had drifted off to sleep. Her heart went out to him as she observed his bruised body and wondered what it was inside Nick McGraw that drove him to play football week after week, year after year, despite the constant pain and chronic injuries that were part and parcel of his chosen sport.

There was far more to this man than met the eye, which was intriguing, because what was visible was undeniably gorgeous. Except for the dark bruises and random scars.

With a slight sigh, Laurel retrieved a pillow and blanket from the linen closet. As she covered his nearly nude body, the feelings washing over her in warm waves were definitely those of a woman rather than physician. She bent down, brushing a kiss against his temple. Then, with one last glare in the direction of the ruckus still going on next door, she wearily climbed the stairs to bed.

NICK WAS STILL sound asleep when Laurel tiptoed by him on her way outside the next morning. A slight smile curved her lips even as she expelled a soft sigh. Nick McGraw was a paradox. How was it she could go from wanting to bat the man over the head with the nearest object to caring for him so deeply all in a span of a few brief seconds?

As she began her daily run through the deserted early-morning streets, Laurel allowed her mind to wander the complicated maze of her feelings for him. She was used to handling men, both professionally and personally. The one thing she'd always prided herself on was her inner strength. Her slender, feminine body housed a core of steel that had enabled her to survive medical school, her internship, residency and a loveless marriage.

However, she was the first to admit she was also a creature of impulsive decisions, most of which had turned out just fine. The reckless lovemaking that had resulted in Danny might not have been a firm foundation for a marriage, but it had given Laurel her son—whom she would not trade for all the wealth in the world. After she'd taken up running to rid herself of the combined stresses of a home, child and medical school, Laurel had impulsively switched specialties from family medicine to sports medicine. And look how that had turned out.

That change had brought her to the sports medicine clinic, and that in turn, had brought her Nick. She grinned to herself as she waved good-morning to an elderly neighbor who'd come out to retrieve his newspaper. Even her piano, another impulsive

decision, had led her to Nick. Or at least to his car.
Her smile widened as she recalled how furious he'd
appeared, storming out of his yard like a wounded
lion. Sparks had flown between them from the beginning.

And that was why, she decided, she was so drawn
to him. Their relationship had started out as a con-
test of wills. Although her feminist nature hated to
admit it, Laurel decided there was something undeniably exciting about being pursued by a man who
didn't know the meaning of retreat.

As she did a series of cool-down exercises outside
her kitchen door, Laurel reviewed Nick's other attributes. He was handsome, intelligent, and although
she had a feeling it was a side of Nick McGraw he
preferred to keep hidden from women, he was actually a caring gentle man. If things were different, if
she wasn't his doctor...

Laurel shook her head, disallowing that rogue
thought. She'd never been one for wishful thinking
and this was definitely no time to start.

"Good morning." The object of Laurel's soul-
searching was seated at her kitchen table, sharing
breakfast with Danny.

"Hey mom, did you know Nick slept here last
night?"

"I knew," she replied somewhat breathlessly, still
slightly winded from her run. "It was too noisy over
at his house.... Hi. How are you feeling this morning?"

He took a bite of toast, observing her while he
chewed. His bright green eyes took a slow tour of
her slender body, clad in a T-shirt and running
shorts, and Nick was reminded of the first time he'd
met her, only a week ago. Seven short days and he
felt as though his life would never be the same
again.

He shrugged, answering her question. "Sore. But I'll spend some time in the whirlpool this morning, and that'll help."

"You don't have practice today?"

"Nope. Generally we have the day after a game off. Then we used to begin with a light workout and work our way up to game day. Although who knows what Carr will think up before the season's over."

"I want to check that knee over before you have another scrimmage," she instructed, picking up a piece of crisp bacon from Danny's plate. "This is good, but you certainly didn't have to cook breakfast, Nick."

He smiled, getting her a cup of coffee. "It wasn't any problem since I would've cooked something, anyway. I was going to fix you a plate and keep it warm, but Danny said you don't eat breakfast."

Laurel took a bite of her son's toast. "I don't usually."

He gave her a stern look. "Didn't they teach nutrition in medical school, Dr. Britton? Breakfast is the most important meal of the day."

Laurel sighed, smiling her thanks as she took the cup of coffee he offered. She sat down in a chair at the table. "I know that. I just picked up atrocious eating habits while I was an intern, and I'm afraid they stuck. Thirty-six hours on, then ten off, then another thirty-six on do strange things to your inner clock."

He rested his elbows on the table, holding his cup between his palms as he observed her thoughtfully. "Were you married in those days?"

Laurel nodded. "Married and a mother."

Something flickered in the dark green depths of his eyes, but Laurel could not discern its meaning. "That must've been tough."

She smiled toward Danny. "It was worth it." Then, swallowing her coffee quickly, she rose. "Danny, make yourself a peanut butter and jelly sandwich and wrap up an apple and some of those cookies we bought yesterday for your lunch. I'm going to take a shower and get ready for work."

"Sure, mom." He drank the rest of his milk in long, thirsty swallows, wiping away the creamy mustache with the back of his hand.

"Oh, and don't forget to put the dishes in the dishwasher," she called over her shoulder.

"I never do," he countered with an aggravated tone. "I do my share around here."

She gave him a smile. "I apologize. You always have and I appreciate it, too."

Danny nodded, carrying his plate to the sink. "I know you do, mom. Like you always say, the two of us make a great team."

Laurel held her breath, hoping Danny wouldn't choose this morning to bring up his idea of inviting Nick into their small family. Her luck held as her son remained blessedly silent.

# 8

WHEN LAUREL REENTERED the kitchen fifteen minutes later, Danny was sitting at the table reading a book while Nick spread a thick layer of strawberry jelly onto a piece of bread.

"What are you doing?" She stood in the doorway, staring at the unfamiliar scene.

Danny's head shot up and a guilty expression flashed across his face before he buried it back into the book. Nick, however, gave her a devastating grin.

"I told Danny I'd make his lunch," he volunteered.

Laurel crossed her arms over her chest. "Why?"

He tore a long sheet of plastic off the roll, put the two pieces of bread together into a thick sandwich and wrapped it. Then he moved to the refrigerator. "Where are the apples?"

"In the vegetable crisper," she answered absently. "I'd like an answer, Nick."

He located the fruit and tossed it into Danny's Mr. T lunchbox, along with the sandwich. He seemed oblivious of her irritation.

"Are the cookies in here?" he asked, reaching for a ceramic container on the counter.

"No. They're in the cupboard to the left of the stove," she snapped.

Nick looked at her curiously. "Hey, you don't have to bite my head off. That *is* a cookie jar, Laurel. The logical assumption would have been—"

"Don't assume anything, Nick," she shot back,

her tone letting him know this conversation went far beyond that of Oreos.

There was a long, uncomfortable silence. Out of the corner of her eye, Laurel saw Danny peeking over the top of his book.

"Come on, Danny, I'll walk you to school," Laurel said briskly.

His eyes widened. "But mom, I can walk by myself. I've been doing it all week." He looked back and forth between the two of them. "I told you she wouldn't like it," he said to Nick.

"So I've discovered," he agreed. "Now what'll I do to get back in her good graces?"

Danny's young brow furrowed thoughtfully. "Whenever she gets mad at me, I usually draw her a picture. She puts it on the refrigerator and I know everything's okay."

Nick cast a wary eye at Laurel. "I'm not certain crayons will cut this one, sport. I think we need something stronger."

"When I was five, I painted Circe yellow to match my room," Danny volunteered. "Mom was looking at me a lot like she is at you right now."

"Terrific. What happened to get you and your mother back on speaking terms?"

"That was the only time she ever spanked me," he recalled. "Then, afterward she cried and said she was sorry."

Nick's green eyes were bright with insinuation as they turned from her son to Laurel. "Interesting idea," he murmured.

Laurel would have had to be blind to miss the sexual invitation in his teasing gaze. "That's enough, you two. Danny, you're right. You can walk yourself to school. I need to talk to Nick."

"Are you going to fight?" he asked with interest, taking his lunchbox from Laurel's hand.

"Of course not," she reassured him. "We're simply going to discuss a few important matters."

"Oh." His small face seemed to actually fall at that and he turned toward the door. Even Laurel's farewell hug and kiss didn't bring a smile to his face.

"Hey, Danny?"

"Yeah, Nick?"

"I think it's going to be a knock-down-and-drag-out brawl."

His face lit up like a Christmas tree. "See ya, mom. See ya later, Nick. Good luck today." He waved goodbye as he escaped out the door.

Laurel turned on Nick as soon as he was gone. "What do you mean by telling my son that we're going to have a fight?"

He leaned against the counter, crossing his long legs at the ankles. "Aren't we?"

"Of course we are, dammit! But I don't want to concern Danny with things that are none of his business."

Nick gave her a long, level glance. "Since I've the distinct impression all this began because I was making the kid a peanut butter and jelly sandwich, I'd say it very much concerns Danny. And if you think he didn't realize that himself, then you're not giving your son very much credit, Laurel."

She pushed her hair off her forehead with a furious gesture, her dark eyes blazing. "Forgive me if I'm not real keen about taking parenting advice from rank amateurs," she forced out between clenched teeth. "Unless you're applying for permanent father status, I suggest you stay out of my son's life!"

"And what if I am?" he roared back.

That question caught them both by surprise. The silence swirled about them, a living breathing thing until Laurel broke it first, sinking down into a chair at the table and looking up at him.

"What did that mean?"

He rubbed his hand over his face, shaking his head. "I don't know," he admitted. "You just got me mad and I said the first thing that popped into my mind."

"I wasn't proposing, Nick," she said sternly.

He gave her a slanted smile. "I never thought you were, Laurel." He straddled a chair, leaning his forearms along the top and resting his chin on them. "Want to talk?"

She glanced down at her watch. "I've got to get to work."

"Call in and say you'll be a little late. I think this is more important."

Laurel couldn't escape the somber green gaze, and even though she knew Dr. Adams would suspect the worst, she nodded.

"I'll be right back," she said, not wanting to use the kitchen phone. She needed some time to gather her scattered thoughts and she certainly couldn't do it in the same room with Nick.

"Fine. I'll make us some fresh coffee."

She managed a weak smile. "I'll say this for you, McGraw—you sure are handy to have around a kitchen."

He returned the smile and feeling a little more optimistic, Laurel left the room. When she returned, not only had he made coffee, but a stack of fragrant cinnamon toast rested in the center of the table.

"You really should eat something," he explained at her questioning gaze.

"I thought *I* was supposed to be taking care of *you*," she reminded him. "After all, I am your doctor."

"And I'm your friend," he countered easily. "I've always thought that's what friends did. Watched out for one another. Made each other feel good."

Laurel sat down and took a sip of coffee, eyeing Nick thoughtfully. They were adults, she told herself firmly. Surely they could discuss sex without things getting out of hand.

"Is that what you call what we were doing last night?"

Nick was standing over her, his expression an inscrutable mask. His eyes were green shields, and it was impossible for Laurel to discern what the man was thinking.

"What do you call it?" he answered her question with one of his own.

Laurel shrugged with feigned casualness. "Foolishness, I suppose." Her hand shook as she lowered her cup to its saucer, the rattling sound unnaturally loud in the morning stillness of the kitchen.

Nick reached out, taking her hand in his, linking their fingers together. His expression had softened. "There was nothing wrong in what we were doing, Laurel. It was natural and right. Which is why we're going to end up making love sooner or later, so you may as well get used to the idea."

He couldn't stop himself from staring at her mouth, remembering the petaled softness of her lips, the incredibly sweet taste. He could feel his body filling with that now-familiar ache.

Laurel found it impossible to think with his gleaming eyes focused on her lips. "You really do take too much for granted, Nick," she protested softly.

He arched a challenging brow. "Kiss me and tell me that."

"Not on your life." She managed to refuse with a light laugh. "I may be reckless, McGraw. But I'm not a complete fool."

Even as her continued resistance made him want to wring her lovely neck, Nick found her valiant effort admirable. He wasn't used to such strength in a woman. It frustrated him, admittedly. But at the same time it also intrigued him. Nick knew the little feminine game of two steps forward and one step back could add spice to the chase. But Laurel was definitely taking things to the extreme; if this was how she usually responded to a man's pursuit, he'd be willing to bet not a lot had managed to catch her.

Nick's expression turned momentarily stormy at the idea of Laurel lying in bed with any other man. He sighed, raking his long fingers through his hair with obvious frustration. This wasn't going well. Not well at all. *Keep it loose, McGraw,* he'd counseled himself, *let the lady know you're not in the market for anything but fun and games.*

"Laurel, how many men have you been to bed with?"

She stared at him. "That's a very personal question, Nick."

He shrugged. "It doesn't matter. I'm willing to bet not a hell of a lot. Like I'm also willing to bet you were a virgin bride."

Laurel rose abruptly from the table, turning her back on him as she poured herself another cup of coffee. "Don't bet the farm, Nick," she counseled grimly, "because that remark just proves how little you know about me. I was a pregnant bride, actually."

His cup was halfway to his lips when she bit out the circumstances of her marriage in a short, gritty tone. Lowering it slowly to the saucer, Nick studied her intently, the lines in his forehead deepening.

"Were you in medical school when you got pregnant?"

She gave him a crooked, self-deprecating smile. "You know, your shocked expression is the same one all our friends gave us when they heard the news. It is, I'll admit, a nice little bit of irony. Geoffrey later used that as an example of one more thing I hadn't managed to do right.''

''The man sounds more and more like a jerk.'' Nick dismissed Laurel's ex-husband with a careless wave of his hand. ''Why didn't you do something about it?'' he wondered aloud.

She sat down again, sipping her coffee thoughtfully, remembering Geoffrey's insistence along those very lines. ''You mean an abortion.... You can say the word in front of me, Nick. After all, I'm a doctor. We don't embarrass easily.''

*And you don't love lightly,* he thought. Vaguely disturbed, he dismissed the idea to return to the subject of Laurel's son.

''All right, as terrific a kid as Danny is, the news must not have come as a welcome surprise. Most people wouldn't have wanted the inconvenience. Abortion *was* the logical choice.''

Laurel frowned into the depths of her coffee. ''Love isn't always logical,'' she said after a pause. ''Besides, it's not that I don't accept the idea of abortion in theory, under the right circumstances. But I never felt it was right for me.''

Nick reached across the table, taking both her hands in his. Laurel tried not to be affected by the warmth his thumbs were creating as they traced litlle circles on her palms.

''You can be a very nice woman, Dr. Laurel Britton, when you're not trying to destroy a man's delicate ego.''

''Delicate?'' she countered with a slight smile. ''Your ego, McGraw, is anything but delicate. In fact, if you ever figure out how to bottle it, I want to buy in. We'll rule the world.''

He threw back his head and laughed. As Nick relaxed, he decided Laurel's reason for resisting was probably due to a desire to avoid any entanglements right now. Her life was filled with enough complications as it was. A new city, a new job, a new home. And something else he still couldn't quite put his finger on.

"May I ask one question?"

Laurel nodded, tugging her hands free as she put her elbows on the table. Lacing her fingers together, she rested her chin on them, meeting his curious gaze.

"I suppose that's safe enough," she allowed.

"What started all this? Why did you get angry just because I was making Danny a sandwich?"

Laurel rubbed her forehead wearily with her fingertip. "It's a little complicated," she admitted. "I'm just a bit touchy these days about my mothering techniques. I've always felt having Danny help out with things around the house taught him independence. When I saw you fixing his lunch, I thought you were criticizing me for not taking better care of him."

Nick's eyes widened, displaying genuine surprise. "I'd never do that. Anyone can see you're a good mother, Laurel. Danny's a great kid; you've obviously done a terrific job."

She managed a weak smile, not knowing how to explain Amanda's theory that a child deserved a full-time mother. She'd been hearing that argument at least once a week from Geoffrey for months. He'd even gone so far as to hint that her career would benefit, as if she'd willingly sacrifice her son for her work. Laurel shrugged inwardly. Why wouldn't her ex-husband think that way? He'd never shown any interest in his son until Amanda had come into the picture.

She realized Nick was watching her with unnerving intensity and forced her mind back to this conversation. "Thank you," she murmured. "Then, there's the fact I'm still worried you and Danny are getting too close. If we were to have an affair, then you disappeared from his life, he'd be badly hurt. He's just adjusting to the idea of being away from his father, although he certainly never saw that much of him when he lived in Seattle."

"Danny said you've been divorced quite a few years."

"Three. But, quite honestly, our marriage never really took." She laughed, no longer finding the memories painful. "Morning sickness did it in."

Nick couldn't imagine not loving a woman who was willing to put up with those mysterious changes in her body in order to carry his child. Geoffrey was not only a jerk, he decided, the man was a fool.

"But why—"

"Why did we stay married all those years?" Laurel shook her head. "I don't know, exactly. I suppose I was far too busy to worry about whether or not I was happy. I had Danny, school, work. Considering the juggling act I was doing with my life, I probably could've signed on with Ringling Brothers."

"And Geoffrey?" Even as he said the name aloud for the first time, Nick hated the guy who'd lived with Laurel. Loved with her. Made a baby with her.

She exhaled a small sigh of regret. "He had his work. You have to understand that no Britton, in the history of a very illustrious family tree, had ever gotten a divorce. Geoffrey's mother threatened to disinherit him if he sued, and quite honestly, I didn't really care one way or another in those days. He was never home, anyway."

"What made you finally decide?" Nick regretted asking the question when her eyes shadowed to a lusterless ebony. The man had hurt her badly. Busy framing her answer to Nick's question, Laurel missed the frown darkening Nick's eyes at the thought.

"Geoffrey fell in love. Amanda's a very well-brought-up lady, a member of the Junior League and all that—definitely not the type to carry on a tawdry little affair with a married man. Besides—" she managed a grim smile "—her father coincidentally happens to be a cardiologist himself, who's built his heart institute to worldwide prominence."

"And who just happened to be near retirement?" Nick asked dryly.

Laurel gave him a faint, rewarding smile. "My goodness, you *are* pretty smart for a jock."

"I like to think so," he replied cheerfully. "Is this fight over now?"

"Why?" she shot back. "Are you suggesting we kiss and make up?" As soon as she issued the challenge, Laurel knew it was a mistake.

Sparks danced in his green eyes as he observed her with unmistakable desire. "I'm game if you are," he agreed. "Just a friendly kiss, of course. Nothing the slightest bit passionate."

"I think I'll pass," she decided, not trusting herself any more than she did Nick. She was an adult, she reminded herself firmly. She could certainly control her body's rebellious urges. It was just going to be a little more difficult than she ever would have thought possible.

"I really have to get to work," she said, picking her purse up from the counter and heading toward the door. "I think Dr. Adams would love an excuse to send me packing back to Seattle."

"Fair enough," Nick said. Laurel enjoyed the light touch of his hand on her back as he walked her to her car. "Will you let Danny spend this afternoon with me?'' he asked as he opened the door for her. ''He's got some crazy idea we should sign Rowdy up for obedience training at the park.''

His grin was boyishly attractive. ''Do you know, sometimes I feel like that kid's the real adult around here? He definitely seems to have all the answers.''

For a moment Laurel was afraid Danny had discussed marriage with Nick, but his friendly open gaze seemed to discount that fear. ''He's seven going on thirty-five,'' she agreed. ''Believe it or not, he was actually born that way.''

''Then you'll let us try to turn Rowdy into a responsible member of society?''

''If it'll protect the rest of my furniture, I'm all for it. You and Rowdy are spending more time with Danny lately than I am. I'm beginning to suspect you're only putting up with me to get to my son.''

Her accusation was leveled at Nick in a light tone, but his answering expression was unnervingly grave. ''You know better than that, Laurel. If I'd met you two years ago... Oh, hell,'' he muttered. ''Forget it.''

Nick reminded himself that neither of them was looking for a relationship with any strings. Both their lives were too unsettled for muddying the waters with any type of commitment. She had her work at the clinic and he had a career to salvage. Even as he repeated those facts to himself, the need to touch her grew almost unbearable. Nick shoved his hands into his pockets.

Laurel managed a slight, agreeing smile but found the effort more difficult than it should have been. ''It's forgotten,'' she said. Then she remembered something that had been tugging at her mind ever since Danny had left the house.

''Do you know why Danny looked like he'd just gotten his Christmas present early when you told him we were going to have a fight?''

To her amazement, Nick appeared chagrined and somewhat embarrassed. "I might," he admitted.

She arched an inquiring dark brow, inviting elaboration.

One hand left his pocket to rake through his hair. "All right. He asked me why you and I argued so much and I told him if people really care about one another, little spats don't mean anything. That if we always saw eye to eye, we'd bore each other silly."

He resisted the impulse to kiss her but was not strong enough to avoid the silken pull of Laurel's velvety brown eyes. Reaching out, he stroked his palm down her hair instead. As his fingers grazed her shoulders, she couldn't hide her slight tremor.

Nick took a deep breath, as if gathering strength. "The one thing you'll never do, Dr. Britton," he promised, "is bore me."

Laurel slid into her bucket seat, escaping the warmth of his hand and the provocative gleam in his green eyes. "I know the feeling," she admitted. Then, turning the key in the ignition she looked up at him, her own eyes displaying her concern.

"I want you to stop by the clinic today so I can examine that knee before tomorrow's practice," she instructed.

"I've got a busy day planned," he protested. "Why don't you just make it a house call this evening?"

"I don't make house calls, Nick. That's one reason I chose this specialty. So I wouldn't have to race off and leave Danny at all hours of the night."

"You made one last night," he reminded her with a wicked, teasing grin.

"Don't look so smug, McGraw," she threatened on a light laugh, shifting the car into gear. "Just wait until you see my bill."

As she pulled away, Laurel caught a glimpse of Nick in her rearview mirror, his hands thrust into the back pockets of his jeans, a thoughtful expression on his face.

"YOU'VE LOST NEARLY eight percent of your strength in that knee," Laurel scolded, after testing Nick's leg strength on the clinic's Cybex machine.

"I prefer to think of it as still having ninety-two percent of my strength," he countered calmly.

Laurel fought down the unprofessional display of anger his stubborn words provoked. She knew that as his doctor she had every right to be concerned about his cavalier attitude. The problem was, the level of her caring went far beyond that.

She crossed her arms over the chest of her lab coat. "Terrific, using that theory, by the end of the season you'll be crawling off the field."

"Don't push it, Laurel," he warned in a low tone. "You've no proof I'm going to continue losing strength at that rate. Hell, the way I've been working out, I'll probably be stronger than ever by the play-offs."

"And don't you talk to me that way, Nick McGraw," she snapped. "I'm your doctor and I think I know more about your body than you do!"

"Not as much as I'd like you to," he retorted. Then, as they glared at each other, a slow smile chased away Nick's aggravated glower. "If you want me to think of you as a physician, Dr. Britton, you should stop looking so enticing."

Laurel didn't answer as she met his unmistakably appreciative gaze. She had met and overcome a great many challenges in her life. But this was proving to be her toughest.

"I think perhaps I ought to transfer you to Dr. Lee," she murmured as she tapped her pen thoughtfully on his file. "I don't believe I can be properly objective in your treatment."

Nick shook his head. "You're my doctor, Laurel. I won't accept any other."

"But Nick..."

He sighed, rising slowly—gingerly, she noted with concern—from the chair. Placing his broad palms on the glossy patina of her desktop, he leaned toward her.

"Speaking as my physician now, just tell me one thing."

"I'll try."

"Do you have any concrete proof that if I continue to play, I'll end up permanently disabled?"

"Of course not. I don't own a crystal ball."

He nodded, his eyes gleaming with a victorious light. "There, you see. There isn't any reason for me not to play."

Laurel knew all too well the athletic mind. The average patient was a consumate expert at hearing exactly what he or she wanted to hear and no more. She wasn't going to allow Nick to twist her answer that way.

"As I said, I don't have a crystal ball. But I do have a file filled with examinations and X rays, and test results that show you're taking a risk every time you walk out onto that field."

Swearing violently under his breath he gave her a fulminating glare. "I'm taking a risk every time I walk across the street, Laurel. That's the way life is. You can't cower behind the curtains in your house and hide from it."

She half rose from her chair, her dark eyes flashing dangerously. "You're far too intelligent to use that old argument! When are you going to quit acting like a spoiled child?"

"And what, exactly, does that mean?" His tone was razor-sharp and electricity arced between them as he held her gaze with the sheer strength of his will.

She refused to back down. "You're behaving like a four-year-old who's afraid someone's going to take away his favorite toy. You're a grown man, Nick, so why don't you just hang up your helmet and allow yourself the satisfaction of having been one of the best quarterbacks to play the game?"

She belatedly realized she'd gone too far as a muscle jerked dangerously along his rigid jawline. Reaching across the desk, Laurel placed her hand on his arm, her expression earnest.

"I know you don't want to give it up, Nick. It's the rare athlete who knows exactly when to quit. Most of you have a tendency to let your minds set dates your bodies can't keep." She took a deep breath, garnering strength. "When are you going to admit that your playing days are over?" she asked softly.

Nick jerked his arm away as if she'd burned it, and Laurel recognized the look in his eyes as they hardened to green crystal.

"When I retire," he grated through tight lips, "it'll be because I want to. Because I no longer enjoy the sport, or because I can't win any longer. But get this one thing through your head, Laurel—no sportswriter, coach or even a doctor, no matter how lovely she may be, is going to make that decision for me."

His harsh expression could have been carved onto the side of Mount Rushmore and his eyes gave her an unmistakable warning. "Is that clear?"

"Perfectly."

"Good." He turned toward the door. "I'll see you this evening," he said as he left. Before Laurel could object, he was gone.

"Burning the candle at both ends, Dr. Britton?" Dr. Adams was standing in the open doorway, his gray gaze inscrutable.

She sighed, deciding it was time to get this out

into the open. She had far too many problem males in her life right now; something had to give.

"Dr. Adams, may we talk frankly?"

He entered the room, taking the chair Nick had just vacated. Crossing his arms over the gray pin-striped vest, he nodded. "Talk away, Dr. Britton."

"Do you object to the way I conduct my practice?"

"If I had any objection, you wouldn't be here," he replied with the air of a man perfectly used to getting his own way.

Laurel admitted to herself that much was probably true. "If you're worried about my professional behavior, you should know that while I consider him a friend, I won't allow anything to happen between Nick McGraw and myself."

"That sounds like quite a challenge, since the man is obviously very taken with you. And you're neighbors," he added smoothly.

Her eyes widened. "How in the world did you know that?"

An expression suspiciously like a smile passed over his face. "Never discount the clinic grapevine, Dr. Britton." Then he surprised her by appearing almost sympathetic. "I know this must be a difficult time for you. Men like Nick McGraw are hard to deal with, even discounting a personal involvement."

"You know what I'm up against, then?"

"The fact that he refuses to accept the idea that his athlete's body may be more fragile than his determination?"

"He refuses to think about retiring. I've tried to point out to him that he's taking a risk every time he walks out onto that football field." Her hands were shaking as she toyed with her pen, displaying all too well her dismay with Nick's attitude.

Matthew Adams's steady gaze held her attention, but there was a warmth in his eyes Laurel had never before witnessed. "It's always upsetting when a patient won't listen to reason, but aren't you taking too much of this onto your own shoulders? Nick McGraw is not your only patient."

He was right. Laurel knew several of her patients would continue the same behavior that had earned them their injuries. Yet she didn't spend all her waking hours and far too many sleepless nights worrying about them.

"I think you should assign another physician to him."

He shook his head, rising to leave. "I'm not going to do that for a number of reasons, Dr. Britton. In the first place, if anyone can get the man to listen to reason, it's probably you. In the second place, you're unquestionably the most qualified doctor on staff to treat an injury of that magnitude. In the third place, as a runner yourself, you can at least empathize with the athlete who doesn't want to suddenly find himself inactive."

"But he's going to end up permanently inactive if he doesn't stop," Laurel pointed out, her dark eyes mirroring her distress.

Her superior shrugged his gray-suited shoulders. "Then I'd suggest you accept that possibility and be prepared to deal with it when the time comes."

This time she knew his expression was honestly sympathetic. "I don't envy you these next few months. However, if you were in another specialty, you'd already have dealt with the reality of losing a patient. While our losses aren't as life threatening as say, cardiology, if you want a medical practice with no risk involved, Dr. Britton, I'd suggest you consider dermatology. To my knowledge, no one has ever succumbed to acne."

He gave her a wry smile that this time actually reached his eyes. "If it's any consolation, Laurel, I feel privileged to have you on staff here. Seattle's loss has definitely been Phoenix's gain."

The smile grew warmer as his gaze swept over her in a far from professional manner. "And I'd still say that, even if I wasn't particularly fond of White Shoulders." With that surprising remark he turned on his heel and left the room, leaving Laurel to stare after him.

# 9

ALTHOUGH IT WAS NEVER spoken of directly, a silent truce was forged between Laurel and Nick. In the almost balmy autumn days that followed, she found herself looking forward to sharing her evenings with Nick and Danny. Practices remained as brutal as ever, and although Laurel could see they were having a detrimental effect on Nick's injury, she forced herself to remain silent.

She had finally come to realize that Nick couldn't conceive of a life without playing this game, even as everything and everyone seemed against him making it through the season. She wished she could help him come to terms with his dilemma, but for the time being, all she could do was tape him up and try to keep him healthy enough to play, while hoping he came to view things more realistically. She didn't want to mar their time together with fruitless arguments.

She gave him daily massages, treated his various sprains and waited for the inevitable. As the Thunderbirds climbed to second place in their division, a play-off spot was clinched.

Laurel amazed herself on Thanksgiving by cooking a superb dinner. The turkey, she thought proudly, looked like something out of a cookbook.

"Wow, mom," Danny exclaimed as he sat down to eat. "This stuff looks really good."

"I had help," she admitted, smiling over the top of her son's head at Nick, who was busily carving the huge bird.

He returned the smile, shrugging his wide shoulders. "It's not that I'm particularly talented. It's just that everyone in my family was assigned various jobs. I usually ended up with kitchen duty."

"Was it neat having loads of brothers and sisters, Nick?" Danny asked. Laurel shot her son a warning glance, but he only smiled innocently in return.

"Most of the time. Although there were admittedly occasions I wished I'd been born a little lower in the rotation. Even after my mom quit work to stay home, I still ended up with a lot of the responsibility."

"Your mother worked?"

Nick laughed, putting some slices of turkey breast onto her plate. "Laurel, any mother with nine children works."

"You know what I meant," she protested. "You told me once she stayed home and did all that mom stuff."

"She worked until I was around Danny's age. By then the McGraw clan was too big to find sitters willing to take us on."

"What did she do?" Laurel inquired, ignoring Danny's expression of protest as she passed him the bowl of sweet green peas. Her firm nod indicated he was expected to take some and with a grimace of distaste, he complied.

"She was an English professor at Columbia," Nick stated, pacifying Danny by handing him an enormous drumstick. "After she quit, she still kept her hand in, working as a free-lance editor for several publishing houses."

"That explains why quotations come so trippingly off your tongue," she commented. "Was your father a professor, too?"

Nick took a Parker House roll from the basket Laurel handed him, smiling his thanks as she refilled his wineglass with crisp Chablis from the chilled bottle.

"Nope. He was a Presbyterian minister."

"Psalms," she guessed.

He grinned. "You've got it. Between the two of them, I can probably come up with something to fit almost every occasion."

"Amazing," Laurel murmured.

"What's the matter, Dr. Britton, are you surprised a football player can read something besides his playbook?" There was a teasing challenge in his tone.

"No. I'm just moderately impressed. What did you do, spend your infancy teething on a copy of Bartlett's?"

Nick threw back his head and laughed, trying to recall the last time he'd felt this relaxed. "Almost. I can't remember our house not being filled with books." He smiled into the golden depths of his wine. "We kids used to play a game to see if we could find a saying that'd stump our folks. We kept a pool going for years, the winner taking all the pennies. Although it wasn't that often that anyone was paid off, I guess the hours spent looking up obscure quotations obviously stuck."

"What did they think about you wanting to be a football player?" she asked curiously.

Nick watched Danny hiding the hated peas in his mashed potatoes and had to stifle a grin of remembrance of his own stubborn youth. Laurel followed his gaze and as Nick's eyes caught hers, they shared a companionable smile. Then he answered her question.

"For their day, I think they were really ahead of the times. While neither of them knew a touchdown from a home run, they wanted me to do whatever would make me happy."

His expression softened and his eyes stared off into space, as if looking back in time. "They were so proud when I got a scholarship to play for USC. Dad flew the entire family out to Los Angeles from New York for my first game.... I still think about how much everyone sacrificed to pay for that trip."

His gaze returned to Laurel. "I've got a nice family. You'll like them."

She smiled, wondering if he'd meant to put it quite that way. There was a formality about meeting a man's parents that signified a certain commitment and the one thing they'd both agreed on was this was a friendship without ties. It had been a casual statement, nothing more, she decided, not wanting to search for hidden meanings in Nick's words.

"I hope you won," she said.

Danny stopped gnawing on the gargantuan drumstick long enough to protest. "Mom! Of course he did.... Didn't you, Nick?"

Nick winked an emerald eye. "I sure did. You know, even with the Super Bowl rings, I sometimes think that was the best game I've ever played."

"Your parents must have been thrilled," Laurel murmured, feeling an adolescent thrill at Nick's dazzling smile.

She loved the way his face lit up when he talked about playing, and hated it, all at the same time. How was he ever going to give it up? The game obviously flowed in his veins right along with his blood. It was as much a part of Nick McGraw as his thick, sun-gilded hair and gorgeous green eyes.

Nick viewed the look of sadness momentarily taking possession of Laurel's face and sought a way to banish it.

"There's a funny story about that," he said, smiling at her. "I'd just passed for a touchdown and the defensive team was on the field when I felt someone tapping me on the shoulder. It was dad.''

He took a sip of wine, his expression reminiscent. ''I asked him what he was doing down there and he said that I'd made mom and him real proud.''

''That's nice,'' Laurel murmured.

Nick's grin widened. ''That's not the funny part,'' he protested. ''All of a sudden I looked around and there I was, standing on the sidelines all by myself. The defensive team had come off the field and everyone was out there waiting for the quarterback.''

''Oh, no!''

''Gee Nick, what did you do then? Did you get in trouble?''

Nick's gaze toward Danny was undeniably fond. ''Well, I didn't exactly get the medal for brilliance that day, but I didn't get in trouble, either. Which was amazing, because as I started running out onto the field, trying to cram my helmet onto my head, I realized someone was running right along beside me.''

''Your father,'' Laurel guessed, her eyes filling with bright tears of laughter.

Nick nodded. ''Picture it: my first game as quarterback of a nationally ranked college team, standing in a huddle, in the middle of the USC Coliseum, with my dad standing there right beside me. I told him he wasn't allowed on the field, that we were supposed to be playing a football game.''

Danny's eyes were wide, his drumstick long forgotten. ''What happened next?''

''Well, when you meet my dad, Danny, you'll discover his most amazing trait is his unflappability. He simply glanced around at the other players, looked up at the clock, and said, 'Oh. I thought you were all finished and had just come out here to shake hands with the other fellows.'''

Sharing in Nick's enjoyment of the story, Laurel couldn't remember a more marvelous day. The only thing that would have made the day even more perfect, she considered as she went to bed that night, was if Nick was lying here beside her. The attraction that had sparked between them from the beginning was steadily increasing day by day and she was admittedly surprised Nick had not made a renewed effort to seduce her.

Laurel had no way of knowing that Nick was as confused as she by his inexplicable hesitation. More than once during the past weeks, he'd picked up the phone to call a woman. Any woman. Just to prove to himself that this yearning he felt for Laurel was merely a simple biological attraction easily satiated by any warm and willing woman. But each time he replaced the receiver to its cradle without dialing. There was only one woman he wanted.

This evening was proving no different, and struggling against an almost overwhelming torrent of need, Nick reached out and dialed the number indelibly etched in his memory.

"Hello?" Her voice sounded hesitant, almost afraid.

"Laurel, are you all right?"

He could hear her expelled sigh of relief. "Oh, Nick. Hi. I'm fine." Her throaty voice curled over him, warm and inviting.

"You sounded upset," he probed.

"I thought it might be Geoffrey. He promised to call Danny today."

Nick glanced at the clock beside the telephone. "With the time difference it's nearly midnight in Seattle."

"I know. He and Amanda probably got stuck at a party, which is just as well. I honestly hoped he wouldn't call." Even as Laurel said her wish aloud, she felt a stab of guilt. She'd watched Danny disappointedly eyeing the silent telephone all afternoon and evening.

"He hurt you that badly?"

She shook her head, the gesture ineffectual over the telephone lines. How could she explain the pressure Geoffrey had been exerting, without giving Nick a far too intimate picture of her life?

"Laurel?"

"No.... I just didn't want any clouds hanging over a perfect day," she answered finally.

"It was nice, wasn't it?"

"Lovely. The sunshine, the dinner and especially the company," she agreed, holding the receiver nearer to her ear, as if she could bring Nick closer with the effort.

Nick didn't want to be alone tonight. Although he'd grown accustomed to spending holidays by himself, today had reminded him of the pleasures a family held on these special days.

"Want to help me build a couple of turkey sandwiches?"

His husky deep tone invited far more than cold turkey and Laurel closed her eyes, fighting off a rebellious wave of desire.

"I don't think so." She turned him down gently. "I have to get up early tomorrow morning." She cast a glance down at the anniversary clock on her bedside table. "This morning," she corrected.

"Hey," he said quickly, casually, "it's okay. It was just an idea."

"A nice idea." Her voice held a soft regret.

"Yeah. Well, I'll see you tomorrow then. Good night, Laurel."

"Good night," she whispered, her lips pressed against the cold ivory plastic.

Nick hung up and walked over to the window, looking up for a long, frustrating time at Laurel's bedroom. Cursing her heatedly and wanting her outrageously, he flung open the liquor cabinet, seeking the numbing effects of Jack Daniel's.

THE THUNDERBIRDS PLAYED their final game of the regular season out of town, and as Laurel and Danny watched on television, she was distressed to see Nick's passing game slowly deteriorate. He had five blocked passes, three interceptions and was given no room to move. Neither did he receive any help from a running game that was shut down with only seventeen yards for the entire afternoon. The Thunderbirds lost to the Miami Dolphins, 16–0, but it could have been 100–0 for all the chance they had.

For Laurel, however, the game resulted in a victory of sorts. Because as the beleaguered offense finally escaped, Nick had been able to walk off, instead of being carried off the field on a stretcher.

Watching the ten o'clock news, she was not surprised to find Coach Carr less than pleased. "I want to apologize to the fans," he declared during the after-game interview. "That team fumbling around out there today was not only an embarrassment to Phoenix and the entire state of Arizona, it was an embarrassment to the game of football."

As he glowered into the camera, Laurel glared back. "But I'm going to change all that. We're having a scrimmage tomorrow at 8:00 A.M. sharp. With full pads."

"In the morning?" the sportscaster asked incredulously. "But you're going to have to fly all night just to get back to Phoenix by 8:00 A.M. Is that really fair?"

"Look," Carr growled, "I'm the one who makes the decisions, and it's fair to me."

Laurel pointed her remote control at the bulldog-like coach, wishing it was something far more lethal as she pushed the button, darkening the screen.

"HI, GOT SOME TIME for a battle-weary old quarterback?" Nick asked with false enthusiasm as he limped into the treatment room.

Laurel forced her face into a mask of professional composure. "I believe we can fit you in, McGraw. How's the knee?"

"Like all those buildings in Venice." At Laurel's questioning glance, he elaborated. "Ancient and crumbling steadily, day by day."

She opened her mouth to answer and promptly shut it, knowing that after that game yesterday and another brutal practice this morning, he was probably in no mood to rehash old arguments. "Let's take a look," she suggested instead.

It took every ounce of her inner strength not to gasp as she proceeded through the examination. "What happened to this thumb?" she inquired calmly, observing it was swollen to three times its normal size.

"Collision with a helmet," he mumbled. "Played havoc with my passing game."

So that explained yesterday's dismal performance. "It's going to take at least three weeks to heal properly."

Nick shrugged. "It usually does," he agreed.

Laurel ran her palm down his side where Nick's skin was turning an unappealing shade of yellow and purple. "And this?"

"Clothesline shot."

"Terrific, McGraw."

"Isn't it?"

She moved to his knee, probing carefully, surprised when Nick didn't flinch. Even he couldn't be that much in control, she thought suspiciously.

"Look over at the wall," she instructed.

"Why?"

"Because your doctor just told you to."

A wary expression moved across his face, but Nick did as he was told. Laurel pulled a long needle from the tray beside her, inserting it into the bruised flesh surrounding his knee. There was no response and Laurel had to restrain herself from screaming.

"You damn idiot," she said in a furious whisper. "You let them shoot you up with xylocaine, didn't you?"

Nick's answering expression was guileless. "Of course I didn't."

She was trembling with rage, at the coaches who encouraged such behavior, the trainers who were all too willing to risk a player's entire future, and mostly, at this moment, Laurel felt like killing Nick.

"Is that so?" she tossed back in exasperation. "Then would you like to explain why you can't feel that needle?"

He glanced down. "You cheated, Laurel."

"No," she retorted firmly, "you cheated, Nick. You cheated yourself when you pulled that stunt. Don't you realize that with your knee deadened like that, you'd have no way of knowing if you were placing too much stress on it until it was too late?"

Nick dragged a hand through his hair and swore. "Look," he argued, "I sure as hell wasn't wild about the idea, myself. But I was in constant pain during the entire last half. I couldn't concentrate, Laurel. I had to do something. It was that or throw the game away completely." His broad shoulders slumped. "So, I agreed to shoot up. It won't happen again."

Laurel was tempted to send one sharp kick at that battered knee right then and end all this nerveracking waiting. Nick was an intelligent man and he'd been around the game too long not to realize this could easily become a disabling habit. Damn him, she fumed.

"I suppose it would be foolish of me to point out that you didn't win yesterday," she observed, not bothering to hide her annoyance.

"Not only foolish," he agreed, "but impolite as well."

With an unfeminine snort of impatience, Laurel withdrew the needle, tossing it uncaringly toward the tray. It skittered across the metal surface with a force born of her anger, falling onto the floor. Neither Nick nor Laurel noticed.

"You could have taken yourself out of the game."

His green gaze turned definitely challenging. "Sure, and let Morgan go in and pull my fat out of the fire?"

For a moment they measured each other in silence. Finally Laurel spoke. "Are you honestly interested in the Thunderbirds winning? Or are you more concerned about the great Nick McGraw regaining his fame and fortune?"

He slid off the examining table, buttoning his shirt as he glared down at her. "That was a cheap shot, Dr. Britton, even for a lady with the fastest mouth in the West. Are you implying I'd risk the team losing rather than take myself out of the game?"

"I don't know what you'd do, Nick. Up until today, I thought you were an intelligent man. That little stunt with the painkiller makes me realize I don't know you at all."

"Do *you* think Morgan could've won that game?"

Laurel shrugged. "How should I know? I'm certainly no expert. I've never even seen the man play."

"He wouldn't have," Nick bit out, "so just get that idea out of your head." A grimace of pain crossed his face as he bent down to tie his running shoes and Laurel's heart went out to him.

"Nick," she said softly. "Let's not fight like this."

He slowly straightened, staring down at her for a long, silent moment. When he spoke, his voice was unusually husky. "You're right. We've made it this far, let's not toss it all away now. Just a few more weeks and I'll have everything under control."

"No more xylocaine?"

He raised his hand in a pledge. "I swear, Dr. Britton, if I see anyone coming at me with a needle, I'll take off running."

"Considering your knee, that doesn't give me a lot of hope."

He bent his head, giving her a quick hard kiss on the lips that sent a flash of lightning sparking through her entire body. Nick felt it, too. He lifted his head, gazing down at her in obvious wonder.

"Wow," he murmured, his finger tracing the line of her upper lip.

"Wow," she agreed breathlessly.

"For a doctor," he observed in a voice that was far from steady, "you sure as hell don't know much about chemistry, Dr. Britton. I thought you've been assuring me this attraction would pass."

Laurel had recently come to her own conclusions about that. And knowing Nick's propensity for un-involvement, her thoughts had been anything but encouraging. She lifted her shoulders in a careless shrug.

"I may have made a misdiagnosis. Are you planning to sue?"

He glanced around the treatment room, grinning wickedly as he found it momentarily deserted. "No, I've got a much better idea."

Laurel's arms went around his neck, her mouth yielding deliciously as they shared a kiss that seemed to go on forever. *Don't think,* she warned herself. *Don't ruin this by analyzing it. Just feel. And enjoy.*

"When I win the Super Bowl," he murmured

against her lips, "will you come to New Orleans and celebrate with me?"

Her answer was immediate, honest. "I'd go to Timbuktu to celebrate with you, McGraw," she said punctuating her words with brief, feathery kisses.

"Oh, excuse me." Tony Lee's smooth apology interrupted them before Nick could renew the blissful kiss. "But you've got an emergency, Dr. Britton. An overenthusiastic volleyball player."

"I'll see you later," Nick said, releasing Laurel slowly, regretfully. "I wanted to go with you when you took Danny to the airport, but Carr's called a team meeting this evening."

"That's okay, I understand." No strings, she reminded herself. No obligations.

"May I drop his present by the house?"

Laurel nodded. "He'd love it." Then she looked at him suspiciously. "I never did ask. It isn't anything that eats Puppy Chow, is it?"

He laughed, a rich, happy sound that banished the last of Laurel's irritation. "Of course not." Then his grin grew absolutely wicked. "You do know a place around here where we can get some oats and hay, don't you?"

"Nick McGraw, you didn't get him a pony?" Danny had been hinting for one, but surely Nick wouldn't be so foolish?

He shook his head. "You know, lady, you sure do get uptight about the litte stuff. See you later." He winked and as he sauntered from the room, Nick felt ten years younger.

All the aches and pains he'd brought into the clinic with him seemed to have been cured by Laurel's very special magic. She was an extraordinary woman, he mused, piloting the Ferrari almost automatically through the streets crowded with last-minute Christmas shoppers.

A man would have to be crazy not to be attracted to her. She was beautiful, strong, intelligent and independent. She was also gentle, loving and so damn sexy that the fantasies she inspired in a man's mind created havoc in his body. Nick grasped hold of that idea, like a drowning man reaching for a length of rope. There had been too many times lately he'd experienced an unnamed twinge of emotion—a feeling toward Laurel that defied description.

It was simply the way she'd forced him to wait, he assured himself, as he pulled the sleek sports car into his driveway. She'd become an obsession and so long as he recognized it for what it was, he could keep his feelings for her in perspective.

The problem solved, he began to whistle "Jingle Bells" as he crossed the yards to Laurel's house, intent on giving Danny his present before he left for Seattle. But the usually jaunty holiday tune sounded hollow, even to his own ears.

THE HOUSE SEEMED so empty. Laurel wandered through the rooms, knowing as she did so she was being foolish. Danny was only visiting his father for the holidays, as promised. Yet here she was, acting as if he'd died. Even as Laurel knew she was overreacting, she couldn't help the depression that settled over her in a black, suffocating cloud.

"Anybody home?" Nick's deep voice broke into her thoughts, but she couldn't find the words to answer.

"Laurel? Did you get Danny off okay?"

Nick was struck by the eerie silence and the total absence of light. She never did lock her doors. What if something had happened to her? That idea made his blood run a little colder and he took the stairs two at a time, oblivious of his bad knee. He held his breath as he opened her bedroom door, expelling it in a frustrated cloud as that room proved as quiet and as empty as the rest of the house.

Danny's room was next, and now that his eyes had adapted to the darkness he could see her, sitting stiffly on the end of her son's bed.

"Laurel? What are you doing sitting alone in the dark like this?" The mattress sank under his weight as he sat down beside her, taking her ice-cold hands in his.

Laurel surprised him with her next action, as she flung her arms around him and pressed her cheek against his shirt. "Oh Nick," she whispered. "Please hold me. I'm so frightened. I'm so horribly afraid."

He could feel her trembling, and as his arms tightened about her, Nick knew he'd give up everything he'd ever worked for if he could banish whatever was causing Laurel this pain.

"Hey—" he lifted her chin, smiling encouragingly "—airplanes are safer than bathtubs. Danny will be fine, believe me."

She shook her head, taking a deep tortured breath. "That's not it."

He tucked her hair behind her ears, the gesture soothingly gentle. Her eyes were as dark and bleak as tombs and Nick felt his heart ripping in two. What was the matter with her?

"But it does have something to do with Danny?" he probed delicately.

Laurel nodded as her shoulders slumped defeatedly. "He's going to stay in Seattle, Nick." Tears sprang to her eyes and Nick watched in admiration as she fought to control them.

He tried to understand. "Danny's staying in Seattle? With his father?"

Laurel nodded again. Slowly, painfully.

"But when was that decided? I thought you had permanent custody of him."

"I do," she said flatly. "But Geoffrey and Amanda want him."

Nick wanted to break in and ask what that had to do with anything. Especially since the stories he'd heard about Geoffrey Britton were anything but complimentary. So the guy wanted his son after all this time. Tough. Nick forced himself to wait, allowing Laurel to tell the story at her own pace.

"Amanda discovered six months ago that she's sterile," she said after a long pause. Her tone was flat, her eyes expressionless as they stared out into the darkness. "They'd been trying to have a child for the past three years and she finally went to a specialist who diagnosed her condition."

"There's always adoption," Nick pointed out.

Laurel nodded. "You'd think that would be the logical answer, wouldn't you? But Amanda feels Geoffrey deserves to have his own flesh and blood."

Suddenly Nick caught the gist of this conversation. He had a sudden urge to put his fist through the nearest wall in lieu of the illustrious cardiologist's face.

"Danny."

Laurel drew a long, shaky breath. "Danny," she agreed in a whisper.

It still didn't make any sense. Why should Laurel be anything but annoyed by the entire suggestion? He probed delicately, not wanting to rush in and cause her unnecessary pain.

"Honey, just because your ex-husband and his wife get the idea in their heads that they'd like your son to live with them full-time doesn't mean that it's going to happen. You've got custody of Danny. He loves you; you're a terrific mother.... I still don't understand."

She dashed at the fresh moisture stinging her eyes, shaking her head in a violent gesture. Laurel was more upset at her atypical lack of control, he realized, than anything he'd said.

"Amanda is perfect," she mumbled. "She's exactly what a mother is supposed to be."

Suddenly Nick fully understood that ridiculous argument they'd had over Danny's peanut butter sandwich. "She's the charmingly competent, domestic type?"

Laurel nodded, giving him a weary look. "Amanda could give Donna Reed lessons."

"So?"

"So, while he's at home, she and Geoffrey will gang up on him and make life so wonderfully perfect, he won't want to come back to me. Nick, he didn't want to come here in the first place, he's bound to want to stay with them."

It took every ounce of control Nick possessed not to tell Laurel that was the most ridiculous thing he'd ever heard. From the bleak expression shadowing her brown eyes, he could tell she fully believed that garbage. What kind of line had that bastard been feeding her for the past six months?

"*This* is his home, Laurel," he said matter-of-factly.

She clung to him, unnaturally cold. "You don't understand." She sobbed into the firm line of his shoulder. "The woman bakes chocolate chip cookies. From scratch."

If Laurel hadn't been so honestly distressed, Nick would have burst out laughing. Instead, he rocked her in his arms, engulfed by a tenderness he'd never before experienced. Staggered by the intimacy of this moment, her grief became his. It tore through him, and as she sobbed harshly Nick's own eyes grew suspiciously moist.

He felt her tears dampening the material of his

shirt, and as he remained silent, wanting Laurel to cry out the pain she was obviously feeling, he realized she'd been secretly fearing this all along, keeping it inside, struggling to deal with it in her own stubbornly independent way. She was too damn close to the problem; if only she'd told him sooner.

Laurel gave in to her grief and fear, loving the strength of Nick's arms about her, the tenderness in his touch, the softly crooning words of comfort he was murmuring in her ear. Not for the first time, she considered how wonderfully gentle he could be, despite his obvious strength. Nick was strong enough to be tender, something Geoffrey had never been. Something Geoffrey could never be.

Laurel slowly felt her will returning. She'd be damned if she was going to allow her son to grow up in the vast wasteland of Amanda's and Geoffrey's marriage. Both of them were too selfish to know how to love.

"She isn't going to have him."

"Of course not," Nick agreed instantly, feeling the change in Laurel immediately. She was going to be all right, not that he'd possessed a moment's doubt.

"I'm not going to allow them to turn his head with all sorts of promises."

"Not to mention chocolate chip cookies," he added with a slight smile that encouraged an answering one.

Laurel tried. "It sounds pretty silly when you say it out loud, doesn't it?"

He took both her hands in his. "A little," he admitted. "But I think your former spouse has been waging a tough campaign lately, sending you on one hell of a guilt trip. On top of all the other changes in your life, it would make sense you'd be a little vulnerable right now."

"You know I worry about Danny," she admitted.

"I know. Just as I know you're a wonderful mother. And he adores you."

Laurel met his gaze bravely. "But he's only seven, Nick. His head can be turned by promises."

Nick's green eyes observed her with gentle censure. "Do you honestly believe Danny is so shallow that he'd trade the love you two share for a couple of cookies?"

"When you put it that way, I guess not."

He kissed the top of her head. "You're damn right he wouldn't. Besides, you've got an ace in the hole, Laurel."

"And what's that?"

He winked. "If you'd told me all about this earlier, I could've told you—I bake one terrific chocolate chip cookie."

Laurel had to share in his laughter, and as she did, the chains that had been gripping her heart during the past six months of Geoffrey's battle to win Danny broke away. The mood suddenly changed as their eyes met, the desire sparking higher than it ever had before.

"Would you do something for me?"

"Anything."

She traced the thin white scar away from his firmly cut upper lip, brushing her trembling fingertips lightly over the chiseled lines of his handsome face.

"Make love with me, Nick," she whispered.

# 10

Nick needed no second invitation. Rising slowly from the bed, he gathered her into his arms, carrying her down the hall to her own room.

The doctor in Laurel tried to make herself heard. "Your knee," she whispered.

He covered her mouth instantly with his own, disallowing another word of protest. When he reached her bedroom, he laid her with an almost reverent care on the bed, staring down at her with unmasked emotion.

Laurel was shaken by the extent of feeling in his flaming green eyes. They warmed her everywhere they touched, from her forehead, across her face, through her plum silk blouse and heather slacks, right down to her toes. She felt the icy chill of her unreasonable dread melting, and with it went any last lingering vestige of reserve.

Nick knelt beside the bed, not feeling the broken pieces of cartilage that usually made such movement painful. His mind was on Laurel as he slowly unfastened the pearl buttons of her blouse, folding back the material with extreme care, as if unwrapping the most precious of Christmas presents. His lips greeted each new bit of creamy skin, and as he blazed a trail of kisses along the scalloped edge of her bra, Laurel shivered deliciously.

"You are so incredibly soft," he murmured, moving over her heated flesh. When his tongue dampened the filmy material covering her breasts, Laurel bit her bottom lip to keep from crying out.

Nick lifted his head, his gaze locked to hers as his tongue soothed the skin her teeth had reddened. "Don't do that," he whispered. "Don't hold anything back from me, Laurel. I want to know what gives you pleasure."

Her liquid dark gaze was filled with desire. "You pleasure me, Nick."

He groaned, reminding himself that they had waited a long time for this and it must be done right. He forced himself to go slowly.

"God, you're so incredibly perfect." He tugged the lace down a bit to allow himself a taste of her fragrant skin. "Do you have any idea how wild I am about your creamy flesh? How wild I am about all of you?"

Laurel's skin warmed and the blood hummed in her veins like a live wire as Nick's lips and hands moved over her, learning her body's intimate secrets. Her blouse seemed to dissolve away, followed by her bra and in short order her light wool slacks, as Nick undressed her with an agonizing leisure. Each new discovery was treated to the same extended exploration, his lips tasting every inch of bared skin as he drew out each exquisite sensation until she felt certain she could take no more of his tender torture.

When his fingers slid under the waistband of her silky bikini briefs, Laurel lifted her hips off the mattress, pressing against his hand.

"Nick, please," she whispered, her voice a ragged little thread of sound.

"Not yet." His warm breath fanned the satin skin of her abdomen, moving downward, following the path his fingers blazed as they rid her of the final barrier. His tongue played with agonizing abandon and as his fingers teased her, Laurel reached out, her palm coming in contact with his shirt.

"Let me," she complained, realizing through this dizzying golden mist surrounding them that Nick was still fully dressed. She was doing all the taking, not giving anything in return.

But Nick caught her hand in his, lifting it to his lips, where he pressed an evocative kiss deep into the center of her palm. Laurel was stunned as the innocent gesture caused a respondent quickening in the most feminine core of her body.

"We've all night," he whispered, shaking his head with a slow, deliberate gesture as he leaned her back against the pillows, encouraging her to enjoy what he was offering.

"Look at this," he murmured on a low groan. "Didn't I tell you your flesh is exactly like gleaming pearls?"

Laurel risked a glance downward, her blood heating to volcanic temperatures as she viewed his wide dark hand on the pale expanse of her stomach. The contrast was jolting, and as she dared to look into the boiling green pools of his eyes, she knew Nick was affected as potently as she.

His stroking touch became more demanding, his lips firmer as they traveled on her body, only to return again and again to savor the sweetness of her mouth. He couldn't get enough of the feel of her, her taste, her scent that swirled in his mind like an inhaled drug, serving to drive him mad.

Laurel's pliant body moved fluidly under Nick's passionate embrace, and if she was capable of speech, she knew she would be begging him to take her now. But as he discovered points of pleasure she had never even known existed, she could only close her eyes and ride the spiraling passion that carried her higher and higher.

When Nick's roving tongue slid up the sensitive skin of the inside of her thighs, Laurel quivered in response, and her breathing quickened as she moaned his name. His stabbing tongue grew greedy, causing Laurel to turn to quicksilver in his hands. She trembled under his touch, crying out as she came to a dizzying, shuddering release.

Nick left her only long enough to strip off his own clothes before returning to the bed, overcome with an attack of pure insanity. His lips roved over every inch of her body, tasting every feminine pore as passion too long suppressed exploded.

Caught up in the escalating energy surrounding them, Laurel discovered her own needs once again as great, her own passion soaring as high and as strong as Nick's. Together they brought each other to the very heights, riding a spiral that carried them beyond anything they'd ever known, out into a universe of their own making where the air grew thin and their minds whirled with a dizzying speed. Just when Laurel thought they'd gone too high, too far to survive, she was flung to a place where the sun exploded into golden shards of light, blinding in its brilliance.

Laurel was unaware of how long they lay there; it could have been minutes, or hours. She was stunned by the intensity of the feelings Nick had unleashed. But even more astounding was the realization that she loved him. Laurel Britton, pragmatic physician, had fallen in love with a man unable, or unwilling, to enter into a commitment. That thought was too depressing to consider and she forced it away, choosing instead to bathe in the warm afterglow of their lovemaking.

As Nick gradually became aware of his surroundings, he attempted to move away.

"Don't," she whispered, her fingers running light trails over the rippling muscles of his back. "I love the feel of you inside me. Stay a little longer."

"I'll crush you," he said, not in any honest hurry to move.

She laughed, a rich musical sound. "That's all right. I know a great sports doctor who's terrific at healing any little sprains or bruises."

His palm ran down her side, delighting even now in the feel of her satiny skin. Nick had believed once he'd made love to Laurel, he'd be over his obsessive passion. But now, sheathed in her velvet warmth, he knew he'd never get enough of her.

"I never knew it could be like that," Laurel murmured, pressing a series of kisses along the bumpy line of a shoulder that had seen more than its share of injuries.

Nick reluctantly left the soft cushion of her body, rolling onto his side, pulling Laurel with him. His hands followed her slender curves, and he smiled down at her. "You're a remarkable woman, Dr. Britton."

She slid her palm down his body, loving the feel of Nick's hard, toned muscles under her fingertips. "You're not so bad yourself, Mr. Football Hero."

Nick felt a renewed desire stirring in his loins as Laurel's hand rested idly on his thigh. He hated to ask, but he had to know.

"Any regrets?"

"Not a one," Laurel answered honestly.

He leaned forward, capturing her mouth in a deep kiss. Laurel met the kiss ardently, her lips greedy as she wrapped her arms about him, willing her mind to go blank. Stunned by her desperate response, Nick felt the earth slipping away.

"Wow," he said as they came up for air. "If that's

your latest tactic for keeping me off the football field, I may just end up spending the rest of my days right here in your bed.''

"If I believed you meant that, I'd take you up on it," Laurel said softly. *Don't push,* she warned herself, concentrating instead on the magic of Nick's caressing hands.

"We could always give it a try," he suggested, his eyes gleaming with renewed desire.

She smiled. "That's what I like about you, Mc-Graw," she said on a throaty laugh. "You're always open to suggestion."

Nick covered her lips with his own, their lovemaking this time gentler and more leisurely but no less satisfying, as Laurel's worries disintegrated like a misty fog under a desert sun.

CHRISTMAS EVE MORNING dawned bright and sunny, a far cry from holidays Laurel had experienced in the Northwest. Nick surprised her by serving breakfast in bed, but she was unaware of what she was eating as her gaze surreptitiously swept over him, loving every rugged feature.

Reminding Laurel more of Danny than an adult who'd already seen thirty-five Christmas Eves come and go, Nick radiated more and more excitement as the day wore on. They spent the day at his house, hanging an eclectic assortment of ornaments he'd collected since childhood on the tall tree he'd saved for them to decorate together. While the three of them had spent hours two weeks ago decorating the massive blue spruce in Laurel's living room, he'd kept this white pine bare, instinctively knowing she'd need something to keep her from dwelling on Danny's absence.

"Where's the angel?" she asked, digging through the discarded boxes.

Nick's eyes were drawn to the rounded curve of her derriere, enhanced by her snug corduroy jeans. She was dressed all in red—a scarlet sweater and crimson jeans—reminding him of a bright, vibrant flame. Her cheeks were flushed, her eyes still glowing from their night of lovemaking. The dark smudges under her eyes added a softness to her appearance, making her appear infinitely delicate and extremely vulnerable. Nick knew that he would remember the way she looked right now for the rest of his life. Years down the road, the image of her so lovely, so desirable, would remain indelibly etched onto his mind.

Laurel was suddenly aware of Nick's intense gaze. She straightened slowly, her eyes searching his face.

"Nick?" she inquired softly, amazed by the warm desire rekindling in her nether regions. How could it be possible to spend all night making glorious, passionate love and still want more? To still be instantly aroused by a darkening glow in those beautiful jade eyes?

She tried again. "The angel?"

He drew her into his arms for a long, lingering kiss. "Right here," he murmured, taking little bites of her rosy lips.

"Ah, McGraw," she said, sighing happily. "You always know exactly the right thing to say. I suppose there are a few definite advantages to having an affair with a man who's had so much practice."

Nick searched for a hidden meaning in her words, looking for some resentment of his admittedly less than noble past. Or a hint that Laurel had changed her mind and now wanted more. But all he received in response was a dazzling smile as she reached up, playing with the errant blond wave dipping across his forehead.

"Back to work," she said firmly. "The tree looks positively naked without an angel on top."

"I don't have an angel. It's a star."

Laurel shook her head on a sigh. "It figures. As long as I can remember, I've always had a fat angel with fluffy yellow hair atop my Christmas tree."

"And I've always had a silver star with twinkling lights," he argued lightly. "Want to fight it out somewhere a little more comfortable? How are you at wrestling?"

"Mats or mud?" she asked, her eyes gleaming as they danced with the provocative idea.

His brilliant green gaze moved slowly down her body. "Actually, I had a bed in mind, but mud does offer a realm of intriguing possibilities."

"Yeah, like who's going to clean the mess up afterward," she pointed out.

"Wise lady. Since it's unlikely we'd find a janitorial service willing to come out on a holiday, we'd better stick to mattresses. Two out of three pins?"

Laurel reached up to press a kiss against his smiling mouth. "At least. But later. The way you keep wanting to play, McGraw, it's going to take us until Easter to decorate this thing."

As they continued working, she and Nick carefully avoided the topics of football or his knee, managing to keep the mood light. Despite their efforts to remain carefree, Laurel couldn't help noticing Nick grew decidedly nervous as the day wore on.

"If you're looking for Santa Claus," she offered dryly, after he'd gone to the window for the third time, "he never comes until all good little boys and girls are in bed."

Nick turned from the large bay window facing the street, his smile devilishly provocative. "That's undoubtedly the most ingenious idea I've ever heard. Want to give it a shot?"

Laurel answered his smile with a warm, womanly one of her own that reminded Nick of the look Eve must have given Adam. She came across the room, standing on her toes to brush a light kiss against his lips. Her fingers began to unbutton his shirt with a tantalizing deliberation.

"I'd say it's definitely worth a try, darling." Linking her fingers in his, she led him down the hall to his bedroom.

Standing beside the wide water bed covered by a dark caramel spread, Laurel resumed her task of unbuttoning Nick's shirt. Tugging it free of his belt, she ran her hands around to his back, pressing into his flesh, delighting in the steely strength of the muscles she found there.

"Laurel," he groaned, attempting to capture her lips.

"Not yet," she murmured, her hands roaming down his sides, and around to his chest.

He repeated her name on a deep moan of male need that Laurel could feel echoed in the galloping of his heartbeat under her fingertips. But she was intoxicated with the effect she was having on him and longed to draw these marvelous sensations out to the fullest. Between each freed button she allowed a long lingering kiss, her tongue slipping between his lips to explore the dark secrets of his mouth. When she finally pushed the shirt off his shoulders, and allowed it to drop to the floor, her hands splayed over his bare chest, her kiss growing more wanton. She twined her tongue around his, playing a little game of thrust and parry until he fell backward onto the bed, pulling her with him.

"Lord, how I want you," he said, pressing his palms on the rounded curves of her derriere as she lay atop him. He moved her against his arousal, and Laurel's breath caught in her throat at the thought she could cause such a fiery response.

"I know," she murmured against his lips, "but it's too soon. Much too soon."

She laughed softly, sliding down his body, her lips

and tongue sampling the mysterious male taste of his skin. Her tongue flicked at the pulse throbbing in his throat, and she could feel its thundering beat treble under her sensuous stroking.

Laurel grew dizzy with an overwhelming sense of feminine power as she rained a stinging trail of kisses over Nick's hard chest and down his firm, flat stomach. She followed the arrowing of golden hair with her lips, exalting in the dark musky taste of his skin, until forced to stop, cruelly impeded by his belt.

Laurel knew this man's body intimately; she'd been tending to it for weeks, she'd lain pressed against it all last night. Yet it had suddenly become unknown, foreign territory she longed to explore. Nick murmured her name with a ragged groan as Laurel unfastened his jeans, pulling them slowly over his hips and down his legs. The palms that delighted in the hard corded muscles of his thighs were not those of a physician, but of a woman, reveling in the inherent differences between the sexes.

He was so strong, so hard; the sinews straining down the columns of his legs were so taut they took her breath away. When her lips replaced her exploring fingers at the inside of his thighs, Nick bucked upward, his masculine body eloquently stating its need.

Even as Laurel's head spun with a heady sense of power, she discovered she indeed was going mad herself. For the more she stoked Nick's flames of passion the more her own blazed a little higher. Her clothes were discarded in a mindless flurry and as she fit her slender body to lie full-length atop him, Laurel was overcome with a devastating need to possess—to be possessed. Desire for him vibrated through her, made her reckless as she pressed her body hard against him, the tips of her breasts stabbing into his chest, her long satiny legs tangling with his rougher, hairy ones.

Nick heard the roaring in his ears and shuddered without being aware of it. Her movements against him were driving him insane; he wanted her to stop before she drove him over the edge . . . he wanted her to never stop.

"My God, Laurel," he muttered, his tongue stabbing into her ear, his hands burning a trail from her shoulders to the backs of her thighs. "You're going to set this bed on fire."

"You can't burn up a water bed." She gave a laugh, a silvery musical sound.

"Want to bet?" As his hand slid between their moist bodies, pressing against her molten core, Laurel gasped. As exquisite as his touch was, she needed more; she needed all of him. Sensing his need and sharing it, he rolled her over, his deep thrusts driving her into the fluid softness of the bed.

Sanity shattered, taking them beyond the realm of thought and reason. Laurel's cries were muffled into the hard line of his shoulder as she crested with an explosive force. Nick shuddered, closing his eyes to the forceful release, feeling his strength ebbing away as he held Laurel close, murmuring inarticulate words of love that neither heard nor understood.

"You have one terrific bedside manner, Dr. Britton," Nick murmured much later.

His teasing words hit too close to home, and as much as she'd prefer putting it off Laurel knew the time had come to broach the subject of Nick's future treatment.

"Thank you, Nick. But I don't suppose you'd make this easier on me and accept Dr. Lee as your physician?"

"Not on your lovely life. I'm a guy who likes to

travel first class, sweetheart. I only settle for the best. In women and in doctors."

Her fingers toyed in the soft blond curls covering his chest. "I can't be sleeping with you and treating you at the same time," she argued softly. "It's unethical."

Covering her hand, Nick linked their fingers together. "Don't tell me I'm going to have to choose between being treated by Dr. Britton, or making love to her charming alter ego."

She closed her eyes to the liquid warmth created by his lips as he pressed a kiss against the sensitive skin of her inner wrist. "Those were the rules from the beginning," she reminded him.

"Ah, but in the beginning you didn't realize what you were turning down," he argued, feeling more anxiety than he was willing to let on. If he had to give her up now...

Laurel was actually relieved to see the old Nick reasserting himself. She could deal with this arrogant football star much more easily than with the tender man who'd not only claimed her body, but her heart as well.

"Won't you just talk with Tony? Do you have to be so stubborn?"

Growing frustrated, Nick hitched himself up in bed, dragging Laurel with him. "I've a right to be stubborn when it's my knee we're talking about. I'll be damned if I turn it over to some quack just because of your ridiculous ideas about who you should and shouldn't be sleeping with."

She shook free, meeting his angry gaze squarely. "Tony Lee is no quack. And I find it fascinating that after maintaining an irresponsibly cavalier attitude all season, you're suddenly concerned about your knee."

His only answer was harsh, rude and brief. As

they remained at a standoff, Nick told himself his anger was due to her intransigence and not a result of any despair on his own part about their situation. He'd finally made love to a woman he'd been wanting for weeks. So why did he feel so miserable?

"Look, honey," he said, trying to find a middle ground, "let's just let things ride the way they are."

Her dark eyes were eloquent in their distress. "But—"

He placed a firm finger against her lips. "It doesn't make any sense for me to change doctors now. There's only a few short weeks left in the season, anyway."

He leaned his cheek against the top of her head, inhaling the wild flower fragrance of her shampoo, determined to remember it always.

Laurel was relieved Nick couldn't see the inner gloom she knew was mirrored in her eyes. She wanted to ask about next season. But that would be presupposing a relationship she had insisted she didn't want. *You went into this with your eyes wide open, kiddo,* she told herself. *So don't muddy the waters by looking for feelings that don't exist.*

"Okay, Nick," she agreed softly. "After all, you're right about it only being a few weeks."

"It's a good thing we're not the type of people to want complications," he said, frowning up at the ceiling.

Laurel closed her eyes. "A very good thing. Someone could end up getting hurt, otherwise."

"But we've managed to avoid that. I think even Danny will be able to accept my leaving."

The pain jolted through her, hot and unrestrained. "You're leaving?" she murmured, more to herself than to him.

It was a rhetorical question, but Nick answered anyway, forcing his tone to remain matter-of-fact.

"This is the last year of a five-year contract for me. Does that make things any clearer?"

It did. Horribly clear. "You don't think the Thunderbirds are going to renew?"

Nick shrugged, wondering why, as many times as he'd been forced to face the prospect of a career move, it had never seemed so bleak as now.

"Sometimes on my good days I convince myself that if I'm indispensable to the team and take us all the way, they'll have to. But speaking as my doctor, would you sign this body to a long-term contract?"

*Yes,* she cried out inwardly. "I can see their point." Her sigh echoed his.

"Hell, I could spend the next five years in five different towns." He looked down at her and his eyes mirrored the hopelessness in her heart. "All the more reason for us to live for the moment, wouldn't you say?" His mouth sought hers, craving release from thoughts he had no business thinking.

No regrets, she reminded herself, flinging her arms about his neck, determined to make the most of the short time they had left.

## 11

"CLOSE YOUR EYES," Nick instructed some time later as they walked across the yards to Laurel's house.

"If I close my eyes, I won't be able to see where I'm going," she pointed out. "I'll probably fall into the pool."

"That's okay, sweetheart, I've always found wet women extremely sexy."

"I'll just bet," she muttered, unreasonably jealous of any women who'd passed through Nick's life before she'd met him. She forced the feeling away, refusing to allow the negative emotion to destroy the happiness she was feeling. *If this is all I'm going to have,* she told herself, *I want it to be as perfect as possible.*

"The pool heater isn't on; do you find women with hypothermia sexy?"

"I always find you sexy," he answered immediately. "But don't worry, I'll hold your hand."

Laurel allowed him to lead her through the kitchen and into the living room. The piquant scent of blue spruce heightened her anticipation of Christmas.

"Okay, you can open your eyes now."

She blinked, her gaze immediately focusing on the most incredible instrument she'd ever seen. "What is that?"

"If you don't recognize a piano when you see one, honey, I think we're in trouble."

Laurel moved as if in a trance, running her fingers

over the glossy sheen of the ebony cabinet. "This isn't just a piano," she whispered. "It's a concert grand."

"I tried to find a twin to the one that shattered, but they don't make ancient old uprights like that anymore," he apologized. "I didn't think you'd have time to refinish any of the relics I did manage to find." He came up behind her, wrapping his arm about her waist. "I was hoping you'd accept this as a substitute."

Laurel shook her head. "I can't let you do this. It's far too extravagant."

"Hey, it was my dog," Nick reminded her. "You were quick enough to point that out to me while surrounded by pieces of mahogany and piano wire."

"But the other was insured. I was going to buy a new one when I got the check from the moving company."

"Lovely, Laurel," Nick said, sighing. "Do you have any idea how much piano one can buy for sixty cents a pound?"

"I can't let you do this," she repeated weakly, her fingers running over the ebony and ivory keys. It had a beautiful tone.

"It's only money, Laurel," he argued softly. "Let me do this for you."

"Nick, I—"

"Try it out," he instructed, pulling out the bench. "I'm told you can't properly judge a piano by its case."

Drawn by the beauty of the instrument, Laurel succumbed, sitting down, executing a graceful glissando up and down the keys. Almost against her will, she began playing a part of Bach's *The Well-Tempered Clavier*, forgetting Nick as she lost herself to the rich, perfect sounds. After she'd finished the brief piece, her hands fell to her lap, her eyes guarded as she looked up at him.

"I won't take it back," he warned her. "I like giving people presents, Laurel."

"My mother always said there were certain gifts a woman could accept from a man."

"I see." His green eyes were bright with laughter. "And what, pray tell, did those gifts include?"

Laurel couldn't help herself, drawn irresistibly to the keys, her fingers played a few random chords as she answered. "You know, the usual things. Flowers, candy..."

"Did she ever specifically say a piano was against the rules?" He pressed his point.

Laurel had to laugh at that. "Of course not."

"Then, we're okay. Please keep it, Laurel, it's no use to me. I can't even pound out a bad rendition of 'Chopsticks.'" He bent down, brushing a snowflake-soft kiss against her lips.

"I still don't approve," she murmured, knowing Nick had no intention of taking the gift back. She managed a teasing smile. "Well, now we definitely have to see you through the upcoming playoffs."

"How come?"

"Because if you don't sign a big contract, you might fall behind on the payments and cause the store to come and repossess it. I'd hate that."

He laughed, as he was supposed to, wondering why giving Laurel the piano didn't make him feel as good as he'd anticipated. The salesman had assured him the Steinway was the most exquisite instrument to be found anywhere in the city. He enjoyed giving expensive presents. One of the nicest things he'd found about money was the pleasure it could give.

He'd also discovered long ago that women were quick to display amazing gratitude for something as easily obtained as a fur coat or a diamond bracelet. That had admittedly been part of the appeal. In fact, he'd planned for this piano to be the instrument of

Laurel's capitulation. But after all they'd shared last night, it suddenly seemed superfluous.

"I suppose you come from one of those families who always open presents on Christmas Eve," she said, smiling up at him.

Nick's gaze was unexpectedly solemn. "Only mom and dad got away with that. They said Christmas Day was for the kids and Christmas Eve was for lovers."

"Oh." Their gazes held and once again there was that flash of heat. "I'll get yours," she said on a whisper.

He smiled. "I've got some champagne chilling next door. I'll be right back, okay?"

Laurel nodded, turning away before Nick could view the unexpected tears that suddenly brightened her eyes. What in heaven's name was the matter with her? Laurel told herself it was just the holidays. Any normal woman who was spending her first Christmas in seven years without her son, in a new town, would get a little weepy. Then, with a deep-seated sense of honesty, she admitted that it was the idea of losing Nick that was causing these atypical feelings of depression. She forced a smile as he returned and she handed him his gift.

"I love it!" Nick's face lit with a huge smile as he sat leafing through the leather-bound set of Shakespeare's plays. He'd told Laurel about coveting his mother's set for years, and she'd been pleased with her purchase.

At first, Laurel felt a little distressed her present couldn't begin to equal his. Then she reminded herself that while her salary was certainly more than adequate, Nick's was in the millions. If he never worked another day in his life, he'd never have to worry about money. Yet she knew that wasn't what was driving him to return to the football field Sunday after Sunday.

"It's a wonderful present, Laurel. Thank you."

"It's not as extravagant as yours," she protested softly.

He drew her into the circle of his arms, punctuating his words with hard little kisses that tasted like champagne. "You've already given me the most wonderful present any man could wish for. I'll always remember these days as the best of my life."

The tenderly issued words brought with them an unexpected flood of anguish. Laurel rested her forehead against Nick's shoulder, absorbing the pain fully, allowing it to course through her, infiltrating her every cell.

This was how she'd feel after he'd gone, she realized with a detached sense of fatalism. Oh, the pain would lessen, but she'd never be free of the dull, aching sense of loss. It had taken root in her heart like a native weed, and she realized that despite all her best intentions Laurel Britton M.D., an intelligent woman with no desire for unnecessary attachments, had fallen desperately in love with a man who definitely shared her independent view of life. It was so ironic she'd have to laugh. Once she got over the pain.

Nick was aware of Laurel's sudden change in mood and realized he'd come dangerously close to telling her exactly how much she'd come to mean to him. *Don't complicate things, McGraw,* he reminded himself. *You were attracted to this woman because she's strong and independent. Don't expect her to change, just because you're having second thoughts.*

"You never did ask me what I got Danny," he remembered aloud.

Laurel's hand flew to her mouth. "I completely forgot." Her eyes circled the room. "I don't see any hay, so it can't be anything too bad." As his eyes lit devilishly, Laurel observed him with genuine alarm. "You didn't get him that pony did you?"

When he didn't answer, Laurel stood up, her hands on her hips. "Really, Nick McGraw, I'm not about to allow you to—"

He silenced her with a hard kiss. "Hey, I know how you felt about that, Laurel. Besides, a horse would make it too crowded around here."

"What did you get him, then?"

Nick frowned abstractly, thinking this was another idea that had seemed perfect at the time but was going to fall flat.

"Rowdy."

A puzzled frown skittered across her brow as her gaze slid to the huge ball of fur snoring happily as he stretched out under the piano. Circe was curled up in a tight ball next to him, her charcoal-colored paw resting on his back.

"Rowdy? You gave Danny your dog?"

"Hell, Laurel—" he defended his present with undue emotion "—he spends more time over here than he does at my place."

"I know that, but—"

He shrugged. "I figured when I moved on, the two of them would miss each other. Besides, I'll probably just rent apartments since I don't expect to settle down for the next few years. That's no life for a dog."

*Nor a man,* she argued silently. Laurel knew Nick's intentions had been good. "I suppose you're right, but why didn't Danny tell me about it when I drove him to the airport?"

He gave her a guilty grin. "I warned him it might be better if I broke the news. I didn't know how you'd take it. I suppose I should have discussed it with you ahead of time, but it seemed like such a great idea...."

"It was a nice thought, Nick," she murmured.

"Don't worry about it. Danny must have been thrilled."

"He was."

They fell silent, both unexpectedly depressed.

"Have you ever made love on the top of a grand piano?" he asked suddenly, trying to break the gloomy mood.

Laurel's dark brown eyes widened. "Of course not."

Nick regarded her silently for a full ten seconds. "I'll be right back," he said, turning as if to leave the room.

"Wait a minute." She reached out to pull him back to her. "Where are you going?"

"To get a blanket. That wood looks a little hard."

"I'm not making love with you on top of my brand-new Christmas piano," she insisted, even as her heartbeat speeded up in response to the seductive gleam in his eyes.

"Oh no?" he mused. "Are you so certain about that?"

She laughed. "I'm certain."

"You know, Laurel, sometimes you can be a very hard woman." He put his hand on her back, bringing her body against his with gentle pressure. His other hand moved between them, delving under the red cashmere until his fingers found her breast.

"But most of the time you're soft, lovely Laurel." He pulled the sweater over her head in a flash, lowering his head to flick the rosy peaks with the tip of his tongue. "So, so soft."

Laurel's protest turned into a moan of desire as Nick's tongue moved from one breast to the other, drawing wide wet circles on her flaming skin until she thought she'd explode from sheer want of him. When he took her fully in his mouth and suckled ravenously, she felt something shatter deep within her.

"Come to bed," he groaned, his lips recapturing hers. Nick's mind was aflame, reason disintegrating. The last coherent thought he managed was the wonder that every time he made love to Laurel, it only served to make him need her more. He was insatiable, unquenchable.

"No," she whispered. "Here. Now." With a strength born of passion, Laurel pulled Nick with her to the plush expanse of blue carpeting. Carried beyond the realm of ordinary time and space, they lost themselves in a December storm that belied the desert sunshine outdoors.

Laurel and Nick remained in a rose-colored world of their own making for the remainder of Danny's time in Seattle. They took long walks in the mellow winter sunshine, holding hands with a comfortable ease that suggested they'd been together for years. Nick took on the herculean project of teaching Laurel to cook, but more often than not the prepared meal would burn, or turn cold on the table as they succumbed to shared desire.

As if by unspoken agreement, they no longer discussed the future, settling for the pleasure they were receiving by living for each golden moment. Laurel couldn't remember laughing or loving so much, and she'd never received such exquisite pleasure from one man's company. Yet despite their carefree attitude, she still backed away from professing her love, afraid such an admission would only revive that uneasy tension between them.

She was admittedly relieved as her son's phone calls became more and more frequent, his homesickness evident.

"I don't think dad and Amanda are very used to

kids," Danny stated as she drove home from the airport.

"Oh?" *Don't pry,* she scolded herself. *Just thank your lucky stars he came home without a fuss.*

"Yeah. I made them a little uptight." A guilty expression crossed his young face. "Especially when I broke the window."

Laurel took her attention from the freeway driving for a moment, sending a quick glance her son's way. "You broke a window? Surely it was an accident."

He colored vividly. "Of course it was. What do you think I am? Some J.D. or something?"

Laurel laughed, reaching out to ruffle her son's hair. "Of course I don't think you're a juvenile delinquent," she responded instantly. "I was just surprised they'd get upset about a little thing like that."

"Well," he replied slowly, "it was a little more than that."

Laurel lifted an inquiring brow.

"I wanted to practice spotting my target when I passed, like Nick taught me. I was throwing the football at this tree next to the house."

"And you missed and it went through the window?"

"Right. It landed on the kitchen table, right in the middle of a tray of those smelly fish-egg things."

"Fish-egg things?"

He shrugged. "Yeah, you know. Caviar. Yuck."

"Oh no. Amanda was having a party?"

"A New Year's Eve party. Gosh, mom, you should've seen it—there must've been four hundred people there. Anyway, this was about an hour before the party started and Amanda got really mad because the gloppy old stuff slid right off the tray down the front of her party dress."

Laurel had to bite her lip to keep from laughing out loud. "I can see where that might make Amanda a bit unhappy, Danny," she responded in a voice choked with restrained mirth.

"Yeah.... Well, then she and dad got in a big fight. She accused him of having a holy terror for a son." He looked at her, his smooth brow furrowed. "Am I a holy terror, mom?"

She reached out, sliding her arm around his shoulders. "Not in the least, sport. I think you're pretty terrific, actually. I'm sure your father told Amanda the same thing."

A flush darkened his face and Danny suddenly displayed an avid interest in the billboards lining the Black Canyon Highway.

"Danny?"

"Yeah, mom?" he answered with what Laurel recognized to be feigned casualness.

"Since you brought this subject up, may I ask what Geoffrey did have to say?"

"He said since the accident was just like some crazy stunt you'd pull, I obviously took after you." The words fell out pell-mell, and Danny looked decidedly uncomfortable.

"Then Amanda yelled back that if he thought she was going to try to undo the damage that had already been done, he had another think coming. I decided about then it would be a good idea to go upstairs, so I didn't hear any more. Besides, the party started soon and everything settled down."

"I'm glad," Laurel murmured.

"You know something?"

"What, honey?"

"They don't fight like you and Nick. It's kinda scary with them."

Laurel shook her head. "Well, it's none of our business. I'm just glad to have you home."

He exhaled a long sigh. "Boy, am I glad to be home." As Danny carried his suitcases into his bedroom, he asked, "Are you going to Cleveland with Nick?"

"No. I don't think so."

Once again she was reminded of Danny's astuteness. "It's because of me you're not going to his play-off game, huh?"

Laurel knew better than to lie to her son. "Hey, kiddo, you just got home."

"I want you to go, mom. I can always stay over at Billy's house for the weekend."

He named one of his new friends. Laurel hesitated. She'd met Nora Bradley at the school open house and knew her to be a friendly, responsible woman with a nice family. But it was not in Laurel's nature to ask favors from anyone.

"I don't know," she mused.

"I'll call him right now," Danny offered.

She caught his arm, making her decision. "No, you unpack and put your dirty clothes in the hamper. I'll call Mrs. Bradley."

"Way to go!" he yelled after her as Laurel left the room.

"DR. ADAMS? May I talk with you a moment?"

Her superior looked up from the medical journal he'd been perusing. "Dr. Britton, your timing is superb. I was just going to send for you."

She entered the office, taking a chair across from him. "Is something wrong?"

He shook his silvery head. "Nothing at all. In fact, I believe you'll find this good news."

Laurel smiled to herself, wondering how anything could possibly make her feel better than she had the past ten days. "I'd like you to consider taking on some additional responsibility," he stated.

Laurel couldn't understand how that was exactly good news, but she kept the expectant smile on her face.

He folded his hands in front of him. "I'm offering you the position of chief of staff, Dr. Britton."

Her head spun as his words sunk in. "Chief of staff? But I'm so new here."

"Length of employment isn't a criterion for selecting a qualified physician," he returned instantly. "Your athletic pursuits have obviously piqued your interest in your field far beyond that of simple professional curiosity. I've yet to meet a doctor with more knowledge of sports medicine than you, Dr. Britton. Now all you have to do is continue putting this knowledge to work in a clinical situation."

"But surely the others wouldn't want me as their superior," she argued. "After all, I am the new kid on the block."

He sighed, meeting her distressed gaze with a level one of his own. "Would it ease your fears in that regard to know that to a man, every doctor at this clinic offered your name to succeed Dr. Parrish?"

Laurel was amazed. "That's another point. I'm the only woman on staff. Doesn't that bother you?"

He arched a pewter eyebrow. "No, why should it?"

Laurel's fingers twisted together in her lap. "Well, I got the impression that you didn't appreciate women doctors in the sports medicine field."

His lips quirked. "Just testing your mettle a bit, Dr. Britton. I had to make certain you wouldn't fold under pressure."

"Are you telling me that I've been under consideration for the top spot since the day I walked in here?"

"Of course," he responded simply. "Dr. Parrish

recommended you very highly, and after watching you work I concur with his opinion. You're a fine physician, Dr. Britton. You combine textbook knowledge with a human touch that's needed when dealing with the ego problems of athletes. You're perfect in every possible way. Now, will you accept, or do you need time to think about it?''

Laurel's impulse was to cry out an unqualified yes. But even though they'd avoided any discussion of a future together, she wanted to talk about the offer with Nick.

"I'd like a few days to think it over," she said slowly. "May I give you your answer on Monday?"

"After the Thunderbirds' play-off game," he said with uncanny insight.

She nodded, feeling the blush darken her skin.

"Of course that's satisfactory, Dr. Britton. I assume you're taking the weekend off?"

She hoped he wouldn't think she was already taking advantage of her offered position. "That's what I came to talk to you about, Dr. Adams. You see, I hadn't really planned until last night to go, and—''

He waved a dismissing hand. "Don't give it another thought. You go to Cleveland, and I'll cover you here."

"You?" She couldn't help staring.

"I *am* a licensed physician, Dr. Britton," her superior reminded her pointedly.

"Uh, of course, sir, it's just that I didn't realize you, that is, I didn't believe—''

"That I enjoyed treating patients? That I much preferred sitting behind this vast expanse of executive desk, wielding the reins of power over one and all?" he inquired dryly.

"I suppose that's pretty much it," she agreed quietly.

"When I accepted this position, I believed it to be

exactly what I wanted," he stated. "Power, prestige and a six-figure income. But like everything else in life, Dr. Britton, there were trade-offs. I found, to my later regret, I rather miss the direct contact with patients."

He smiled encouragingly. "Fortunately for you, the chief of staff still maintains a patient load, although it's admittedly less than you have now. I assure you, however, the cases will be far more challenging and your surgery schedule will definitely increase. You're much too talented to be putting ice on minor sprains."

He rose, holding out his hand, indicating to Laurel their meeting was over. "I'm looking forward to returning to the treatment room this weekend, Doctor. And give my best wishes to Mr. McGraw. If the weather forecast is accurate, he'll need all the help he can get."

## 12

"MY GOD," Laurel gasped, rubbing her gloved hands together, "how cold is it out here?"

"Officially one degree below zero," the fan wearing a bright, knitted scarf and cap next to her ground out. "But with this wind, I'd guess the windchill factor is probably somewhere around a million below."

She shivered, glancing around the stadium at the crowd of over 77,000 intrepid sports fans wrapped in a variety of outer garments. When a tractor came out onto the field, scraping away a sheeting of ice and snow, Laurel's heart froze along with the rest of her body. It would be an absolute miracle if Nick's knee survived playing on that icy field.

Making a decision, she marched down the concrete steps, coming up behind the short, stocky Coach Carr. He turned as she tapped him on the shoulder.

"Hey, lady, no broads allowed on the bench."

"I am not a broad, Mr. Carr," she said, her voice coated with icicles. "I'm a sports physician. Dr. Laurel Britton."

"Good for you," he grunted. "Now you'd better get off the field before I call security."

"Hey, I know her." An assistant coach suddenly made the connection. "This is McGraw's doctor. The one from the clinic."

Coach Carr's eyes were beady little marbles as they raked over Laurel's face. "You're kidding."

Laurel fought down the anger created by his derisive tone. "I'm Nick McGraw's physician," she stated firmly. "And since there's a distinct possibility of his being injured today, I'm staying here on the sidelines."

"We don't allow girlfriends on the sidelines." He turned away. "As for medical treatment, we've got trainers here."

Laurel grabbed his arm, jerking him about to face her with a force that would amaze her later. "Trainers that'll shoot him full of xylocaine. On that icy field, with a numb leg, he'd be bound to lose his footing," she retorted furiously.

"McGraw's a big boy. If he wants a shot, we're not going to go to his mama for permission. Or his girlfriend."

Laurel felt like slapping his face, but restrained the impulse, knowing it would do no good. She put her hands on her hips and looked the man directly in the eye.

"Look, I'm his doctor, and I'm staying. If you don't like that, Coach Carr, then you're going to have to have me arrested and hauled from the field, because that's the only way I'm leaving."

Her dark eyes flashed dangerously, boring like lasers into his face. Obviously deciding he'd met his match, the coach shrugged uncaringly. "Hey, if you want to give up a good seat, it's your business." Then he waved an ungloved finger in her face. "But if you say one word to any of my players I'll take you up on that offer. Understand?"

Laurel nodded.

He shook his head, turning away. "Broads. Who can figure them?"

The game was a comedy of errors from the start. In the course of the first nineteen plays, there were seven turnovers, as player after player fumbled the ice-coated pigskin.

"Watching these guys is like going to the dentist," mumbled a television cameraman standing next to Laurel.

"It's not pretty," she agreed, cringing as Nick disappeared under a pile of Cleveland players.

"Hell, it's downright ugly," he protested, focusing on the play. "This is not the way the game was meant to be played."

The ball popped loose, Cleveland recovered and as Nick limped slowly off the field, Laurel noted he had snow for hair and ice for eyes. As the fumbles and miscues became commonplace, the intensity on the field increased. Frustration and cold were making tempers short as the ball continued to bounce off numbed fingers. Laurel had to cover her mouth with her hand to keep from crying out as Nick was hit again.

"If Cleveland wins, they're going to call that the blitz that killed Phoenix," the cameraman said, wincing as the mountain of bodies on top of Nick increased.

"This is the worst thing I've ever seen," she objected. "Why doesn't someone do something?"

The man shrugged. "Hey, that's what the Browns have been saying they were going to do all week. Their entire game plan was to worry McGraw with an exotic set of blitzes. They know his knee can't take much abuse, especially on that frozen surface."

"They're purposefully trying to injure him?" Laurel wondered who'd misnamed this sport a game. What was happening out on the field was definitely a war.

The cameraman gave her a strange look. "Sure. With the defense aimed at McGraw, he won't be around by the end of the game. Morgan hasn't had much playing time all season, so he'll be cold.... Well, that's the half," he said as the buzzer sounded.

Laurel knew there was no believably professional reason for her to invade the locker room. She crossed her frozen fingers, said any number of small prayers and paced the sidelines, wishing for the game to be over.

Cleveland came out in the second half more determined than ever to put pressure on Nick. "The Thunderbirds have been pulling weird stuff out of their bag of tricks all season," the opinionated cameraman muttered as he followed the play downfield. There was a resounding crash of helmets as Nick went down again. "Looks like they emptied their bag to get here."

"If you're such an expert," Laurel snapped, tired of his constant sarcasm, "then why don't you just put that camera down and go out there and try it for a few minutes?"

He stared at her, his frost-tinged lashes blinking his surprise. "Hey, lady, don't get uptight. I didn't mean anything."

But Laurel failed to hear his apology, her attention directed once again to Nick. Amazingly, he completed two short passes, and handed off twice more, moving the ball down the field in a series of successful plays. Calling time, he jogged to the sidelines, where Ward Carr was waiting.

"Okay, McGraw, here's your chance to redeem yourself," the coach said. "I want to hit Richardson in the end zone."

Laurel could hear the exchange and didn't miss the surprise in Nick's voice. "You're going with the pass?"

"Hell yes, we're going for all the marbles on this play."

"It's only the third quarter," Nick argued.

"Look, McGraw, if you don't want to be pulled right now, execute the play I've just called. You may be the guy making the big bucks, but I'm the coach. Understand? Now get out there, and if nobody's open, throw the damn ball into Lake Erie."

When several heads bobbed up out of the huddle a minute later to look incredulously at the sidelines, Laurel realized Nick was not alone in thinking the play risky. Not expecting it, Cleveland wasn't prepared and Nick's receiver was able to catch the ball in the end zone. He took several steps with it before a Cleveland player came in from behind and chopped it out of his hands.

When the official ruled "no catch," the fans in the stadium went wild, but Laurel didn't notice. Her attention was riveted on Nick, who'd gone down on a late hit. He wasn't getting up, and the team trainer had run out onto the field.

"Well, looks like the miracle comeback quarterback just flat ran out of miracles," the cameraman observed, directing his lens toward the action.

"Is he moving his leg?" she asked, wanting to hit the man for his heartless remark, but realizing he was able to see far more with his telephoto lens than she could.

"Nope. They just tried bending it, and he looked like he was going to pass out," he related. "He's out for the day."

"If it's what I think it is," she said with a sigh, fighting back unprofessional tears, "he's out, period."

She followed the stretcher out onto the field. Nick was propped up on his elbows, eyeing the scoreboard incredulously. "What in the hell's going on here? What do they mean no catch?" As he attempted to struggle to his feet, both the trainer and Laurel pushed him back down.

"Nick, you can't put any weight on that knee until I have a chance to examine it," she protested.

"That's a fair catch, dammit!"

"That's not the point right now."

He turned his blazing glare directly on her. "The hell it isn't!"

He was still blustering about the injustice of it all as they wheeled him into the emergency room of a nearby hospital and continued until the painkiller she prescribed finally knocked him out.

It was dark when Nick woke up much later. He looked around, trying to remember where he was. Oh God, he thought. The memory of the game was coming back.

"Laurel?"

She rose from the chair beside his bed, bending down to press a light kiss against his temple. "I'm right here."

"Did we lose?"

Dear Lord, she wondered, how could he care right now? She nodded. "I'm afraid so. It was a ridiculous day for football. The Thunderbirds couldn't help losing."

"It was a ridiculous day for the Browns, too. And they won," he reminded her. He linked his fingers behind his head. "Well, I suppose that's that. At least now we don't have to get me back on my feet for the Super Bowl. We've got the whole off-season to build my knee back up."

Laurel said nothing, knowing denial was often the first response of anyone facing an unpleasant medical fact.

Nick's head felt surrounded by a dense fog and his mouth was dry. He reached out for the glass of water beside the bed, thanking Laurel with his eyes as she held it for him.

"I'm glad you came," he murmured. "I wouldn't have wanted to entrust my body to just any old quack."

Laurel managed a smile. "I'm not wild about you entrusting that body to anyone other than me, McGraw. I've got first dibs."

Nick returned the smile with a weak one of his own. "What did you prescribe down in that emergency room, anyway? I feel like I'm floating somewhere out in space."

"Close your eyes and you won't be so dizzy," she instructed.

He did as she said. "Hey, this is kinda nice. If you're into flying merry-go-rounds."

Laurel bent down to kiss him. "Go to sleep, darling. I'll be here when you wake up."

Laurel called Danny, assuring him Nick would be just fine. Nora Bradley got on the line to say Danny was no trouble, and was welcome to stay as long as he wished. Her next call was to the clinic.

"Is it what we feared?" Matthew Adams asked.

"Yes, the damage to the tendons is extensive, and the cartilage is just lying in ruins." Tears welled up in her eyes and Laurel sniffled inelegantly, blowing her nose.

"Well, that's that," he replied after a long silence.

"That's that," she agreed flatly. "I'm bringing Nick back to Phoenix the day after tomorrow."

"Does he know?"

Laurel sighed. "I'm sure he must. I haven't said anything, but the man's been an athlete long enough to be well acquainted with what his body can and cannot do. Besides, he's always known the risk."

"That he has," the older man agreed. "Have a safe flight back, Dr. Britton."

"Thank you," she murmured. She went downstairs once again to X ray, studying the films carefully, determined to be able to give Nick as much encouragement about his prognosis as possible. It didn't look at all good, she decided. But it could have been a lot worse. And that was what she was going to have to make him understand.

"HI," NICK GREETED her as she entered the room before noon. "You're just in time for the news. Want to watch the report of yesterday's debacle?"

Laurel shook her head. "Not really. But I don't suppose we have any choice?"

"Nope. I never did get to see that touchdown pass they stole from me." He managed a smile. "I knew I was in trouble when I looked up and saw that monster blocking out the sun."

They viewed what the sportscaster was calling highlights of the game, although Laurel considered them badly labeled. Neither team had distinguished itself, the weather proving a much tougher opponent.

"Hell yes, I have to blame McGraw." Coach Carr came onto the screen, his face set in a scowl.

"It was a team loss," the sportscaster pointed out. "McGraw actually played quite well, considering the circumstances."

"McGraw makes the most money; he's well paid to perform."

"Is it true that last hit ended his playing days?"

As Laurel sat on the edge of his hospital bed beside him, she felt Nick tense, but he remained silent.

"That's what they say."

"What does that mean to next year's Thunderbirds?"

"I don't believe the myth about needing a veteran quarterback."

Nick only grunted as they wrapped up the interview. Then Laurel's clinic came onto the screen.

"We're here with Dr. Matthew Adams, administrator for the Phoenix Sports Medicine Clinic, where Nick McGraw has been receiving daily therapy for an injury suffered last season," the reporter announced. "Dr. Adams, is it true that Nick's physician is in Cleveland with him at the moment?"

"That's right. Our chief of staff, Dr. Britton, has examined Mr. McGraw and will be returning to Phoenix with him tomorrow."

"Chief of staff?" Nick asked, looking at Laurel with obvious surprise. "When did that happen?"

"It's a long story," she murmured, reaching for the remote control before Adams could continue. "And the announcement is definitely premature. I haven't accepted it yet."

He held the control out of her reach. "But you've been offered the post."

Laurel nodded. "A couple of days ago. Let's turn it off."

"Wait a minute, they're talking about you, Dr. Britton."

"And Dr. Britton's prognosis about his future?" the reporter asked.

"I'm afraid Nick McGraw's playing days are over."

Nick froze and Laurel risked a tentative glance in his direction. "Nick," she began softly.

The television screen darkened as he pointed the control in its direction. "Is that what you told him?" His voice was under tight control.

"Let me explain."

As he flung her hand off his arm, his eyes were expressionless. "I asked you a question, Laurel. Is that what you told him?"

"Yes." It was a whisper, but Nick had no trouble hearing it in the swirling silence of the room.

"I see. Is that your best guess? Or are you positive?"

"Positive. But you'll be able to walk, Nick," she rushed to add.

"Walk. But no football."

She shook her head. "No, no football."

"They told me that last year," he reminded her.

"That was different. Dr. Phillips only said he wouldn't recommend it. He didn't say it was a total impossibility. Believe me, there's no way your knee will be able to sustain any more hits. And it isn't flexible enough to allow you the mobility you need out on the playing field."

"That's your opinion."

"That's my opinion," she agreed.

"I'm requesting a consultation with another specialist," he stated firmly, crossing his arms over his chest.

Laurel understood his reasoning and welcomed it. She didn't want him to ever wonder if she'd lied, in order to get him to stop playing.

"I think that's a good idea. Anyone in particular?"

He shook his head. "No. I'll let you choose. So long as you promise not to stack the deck against me."

Laurel bent down, kissing Nick with all the love she held for him in her heart. "I promise," she pledged.

She arranged for the extensive examination the day after they returned to Phoenix. She wanted Nick to accept the full extent of his injury as soon as possible, so he could get on with his life.

"Well, I guess that's about it," he commented flatly, alone with Laurel after the famed sports physician she had brought in from Boston had confirmed her diagnosis.

"I'm afraid so," she agreed softly. 'Nick, I'm truly sorry."

"Not as sorry as I am." He laughed hollowly. "I should've known it would never work out."

"You managed to play the entire season," she pointed out. "Against incredible odds."

"Believe it or not, I wasn't talking about football, Laurel. I was talking about us."

"Us?"

"The chief of staff and the washed-up jock."

The finality in his low tone frightened Laurel. "What do you mean? Why should this change anything between us?"

"You're the lady who didn't want complications."

"So I've changed my mind." She decided to take a chance. "And I think you have, too."

His gaze swept over her. In the dark, linen shirt-waist dress and pumps she looked every inch the successful professional woman. The hoops in her ears as well as her watch and stickpin were simply fashioned in gold, but expensive. This was a woman with her life on track. She'd faced odds that had equaled his own right now and succeeded. Admirably. And more important, she'd done it on her own. The one thing Laurel Britton didn't need was to be saddled with his problems. For a time their lives had run a parallel course, but now hers was rocketing skyward, while his had fizzled and was crashing down toward earth.

"Look, Laurel, you've got the world in the palm of your hand right now. Chief of staff—"

"I haven't accepted that," she interrupted.

"You will," he overrode her firmly. "Your career is booming, and now that Geoffrey and Amanda have changed their mind about wanting to share their perfect home with a spirited young boy, you don't have any more worries about Danny.

"You're intelligent, lovely and, quite honestly, the most lovable as well as loving woman I've ever met. You're going to have the guys lining up outside your door in droves, sweetheart. The last thing you need is an aging, battered old has-been.''

"Don't you dare talk that way about the man I love,'' she protested heatedly. It was the first time the word had been spoken aloud and its importance reverberated around the room as Nick and Laurel observed each other for a full minute. Nick finally broke the heavy silence.

"You don't love me.'' He groaned unconsciously as he slowly slid off the examining table, accepting the cane she offered him with a grim expression. "You're just confusing love with pity, Doctor. You're going to have to learn to maintain a more professional attitude.''

"Nick…'' Laurel reached out, but he shook free of her arm.

"Let it go, Laurel,'' he pleaded. "I'm just not any good for anyone right now. Don't you see, I'm not in any position to be making any decisions.''

"Don't you understand?'' Tears ran unchecked down her cheeks as she remained unaware she was weeping. "I fell in love with you in spite of the fact that you played football. Not because you did.''

"It's who I am,'' he objected firmly. "All my life, I've thought of myself as a football player. My entire life. I can't separate the two, Laurel, and I've never wanted to.''

He drew a long, painful breath. "I'm intelligent enough to realize there's no way in hell I'm ever going to play the game again. So obviously I can't offer you anything.''

He reached out his free hand, brushing her hair from her face, tucking it behind her ear in a heartbreakingly familiar gesture.

"Laurel, do me a favor.''

"Anything.''

"Don't love me. I really can't handle that right now, and it's definitely not fair to you."

Laurel was angry and desperate as she saw their life together slipping away like grains of sand through open fingers. "Don't tell me what's fair and not fair. And you've no right to tell me who I can and cannot love."

As she lifted a tear-stained face to his, Nick's fingers moved over her delicate features, as if the memory of her would have to last him a lifetime.

"Be good to yourself," he said gruffly, turning away, his own eyes unnaturally moist.

Laurel couldn't believe he was actually going to go until she watched the black Ferrari pull out of the parking lot and disappear around the corner. He was gone, her brain echoed hollowly. Just like that, he'd driven out of her clinic and out of her life.

# 13

LAUREL KEPT ABREAST of Nick's progress for the next two weeks through Danny, as her son visited his house every day. She waited for a message that he asked about her, wanted her, anything. But he seemed determined to make their break permanent, only keeping his promise not to hurt her son.

She was also hurt, but not surprised, when the consulting physician she'd brought in from Boston telephoned, letting her know he'd scheduled Nick for some minor-repair surgery. Nick didn't even want her as a doctor any longer. Laurel knew he was purposely remaining as cold and distant as possible, in an attempt to persuade her not to love him. But he might as well have attempted to stop the sun from rising every morning.

On Super Bowl Sunday, Laurel watched two teams, neither of which she cared anything about, battle throughout the afternoon. Knowing how much this game had meant to Nick, she was unable to expunge the mental image of him watching the game in his self-imposed isolation. It had to be extremely painful for him, knowing that he'd never again play the game that his entire life had revolved around.

She rose from her chair, going over to the window, staring at his house for a long, silent time. The man was so damnably frustrating, she seethed inwardly, thinking back over Nick's behavior. He was arrogant, stubborn and incredibly shortsighted. And stupid. Because he hadn't understood how much he meant to her; how deeply she loved him.

Suddenly, Laurel knew what she had to do. The answer hit her with all the crystal clarity of a spring-fed mountain stream.

"I'm going next door," she said to her son, who was still engrossed in the action taking place on the television screen.

Danny turned his attention from the game momentarily. "It's about time," he said simply. As Laurel pulled the bottle of champagne she'd been saving out of the refrigerator, Danny called out from the family room. "Hey, have fun. And don't worry about me. I'll microwave something for dinner."

She looked around the doorframe. "Am I ever glad your father never realized what a prize you are, kiddo."

He grinned a little self-consciously, a blush spreading out under the freckles. "Ah gee, mom, you know I'd never live with him and Amanda. They don't love each other like you and Nick. We're going to have a neat-o family, huh?"

From the mouths of babes. "Absolutely neat-o," she agreed.

She walked across their backyards, making her way to Nick's back door. "Hi Rowdy," she whispered, as the huge golden retriever came bounding into the kitchen, sliding on the rug, his feet almost going out from under him in his eagerness to greet Laurel.

Danny had returned the dog to Nick, insisting Nick needed company, and Laurel had been surprised to find she actually missed the friendly beast constantly underfoot. She held the bottle high above her head as he placed his huge paws on her shoulders and vigorously began washing her face.

"Rowdy?" Nick called out. "What's going on in there?"

Laurel pushed the dog down, smoothed the front of her sweater and took a deep calming breath. Then she made her way bravely toward Nick's den.

"He was saying hello to a neighbor," she said simply.

Nick's eyes widened and he felt as if his heartbeat had suddenly trebled its rate. "Laurel, what are you doing here?" He quickly got up out of his chair.

She reached down and flicked off the television. "I've come to seduce you, Nick."

"Laurel—"

She wasn't about to give him an opportunity to object. "See, I've even brought champagne." She gave him a breathtakingly beautiful smile as she handed him one of the stemmed crystal glasses. "I've never been terribly good at this, but I think it's about... ah, there it goes." She nodded her approval as the cork popped with the retort of a rifle shot.

Ignoring Nick's questioning gaze, she poured some effervescent champagne into both glasses, lifting hers in the gesture of a toast.

"To strings," she murmured. "And celebrations."

Nick stared down into her shining face. Lord, she was so beautiful. "May I ask what we're celebrating?"

"Why, our upcoming marriage," she answered, her eyes guileless. "I lied, Nick. I want a lifetime of loving, glorious complications." She dipped her finger into the champagne, lifting it to the harshly cut line of his lips, wetting them with the icy liquid.

"Laurel," he protested on a weak ragged note, attempting to maintain a semblance of sanity as her finger worked its way between his lips. Her eyes were dark black pools, drawing him deeper and deeper into their depths, and suddenly Nick realized what it must feel like to be drowning in quicksand. He put his glass down slowly onto the table.

Moaning a soft oath, he lowered his head, his mouth capturing hers. His fingers thrust through her hair, holding her to a suddenly savage kiss that was naked in its need. Laurel was staggered by the intensity of his lips but even more stunned by her own, as they moved desperately under his. Neither noticed as her glass dropped to the carpet, spilling a trail of golden liquid that Rowdy happily lapped up.

"I'm not leaving here until you make love to me, Nick McGraw," Laurel said, her lips plucking at his as she punctuated her words with hard little kisses. "Then I dare you to tell me that you don't want to spend the rest of our lives together."

Nick wanted to take her to bed right then. But there was something he had to take care of first. He forced his mind to the words he'd been rehearsing all morning.

"There's nothing I'd like better than spending the rest of our life in carefree decadence," he began, his hand moving over one cashmere-clad breast.

Laurel felt that familiar stirring as his fingers plucked idly at the hardening tip. "Mmm. I think that sounds like a perfect idea."

"Unfortunately, I do have other obligations." The roving hand slid under her sweater, and his palm cupped intimately.

Laurel was finding words more and more difficult. "Why do I have the feeling you're trying to tell me something?"

"I don't know. What could I possibly have to tell you except that I've got a new job?" He lowered his head, his breath warming her skin through the wispy material of her bra.

Laurel pulled his head up by his blond hair. "A job? What job? When? Where? Not in football? Did you take it?"

He laughed. "Hey, slow down. Which of those questions do you want answered first?"

"When? And why didn't you tell me?"

"I accepted it this morning and have been working up my nerve all day to make that long trek next door. I suddenly realized I didn't know what I'd do if you told me to get lost."

There were little seeds of worry in his green eyes that Laurel hastened to dispel. "Never," she said instantly, pressing a hard kiss on his lips. "Where?" She held her breath.

"Phoenix."

So far so good. "In football?"

He shrugged. "In a way. I'll be directing a YMCA winter youth league. My main responsibility will be training the volunteer coaches to make certain the boys have fun. Everyone gets to play, and there's less emphasis on winning at all costs compared to some of the other programs available."

His expression grew earnest. "Despite my reluctance to retire, I've been giving the whole thing a lot of thought the past few months. I didn't want to sell cars, or open a restaurant or even try sportscasting like so many other ex-jocks. I've no inclination to go to Hollywood, and I hate the idea of people using me to push deodorants and shaving cream....

"But I like the idea of this, Laurel. And I think I can do a good job."

"I know you can," she said with heartfelt conviction. "You'll be wonderful. Terrific. In fact, you'll be the best coach those kids will ever have and someday we'll be watching your players in the Super Bowl." Her enthusiasm for the idea escalated. "Isn't that an incredible thought? Just think of it—"

She was just getting wound up when Nick pressed his fingers against her lips. "Laurel?"

"Yes?"

"I thought you'd come here to seduce me," he reminded her on a deep, husky note. The lambent heat in his darkening jade eyes told its own story.

"Oh yes," she whispered, going up on her toes to press her lips against his. "And don't you dare try to argue with me, McGraw, because I'm not taking no for an answer."

"Lovely Laurel," Nick groaned as she fit her curves to his body. His lips met hers in a heated demand, rekindling the fires he'd tried to keep safely banked these long and lonely days.

Every vestige of restraint fled as Laurel gave herself fully to Nick's ravenous kiss, her fingers desperately at the buttons of his shirt. She had to touch him, had to know that his skin flamed for her, just as hers was on fire for him.

"Oh yes," he encouraged, closing his eyes to the feel of her fingertips against his moist skin. He moaned his pleasure as she dragged her lips from his to taste of his tangy flesh.

The taste, that marvelous male taste of his hard chest that she'd not been able to exorcise from her memory, only had her wanting more. His belt. It had to go, she couldn't bear it any longer. She had to reestablish her claim over all of this man who'd scorched away reason and made her a prisoner of her own blazing need.

She lifted her arms in mute assistance as he tugged her red sweater over her dark head. The wispy scarlet bra followed and his mouth moved hungrily to her breast, his teeth tugging at a rosy erect nipple, causing Laurel to cry out.

"I want to be gentle with you, to go slowly," he groaned, burying his head in her yielding softness.

Laurel clung to him, her hips moving against his, kindling fires that were raging wildly out of control. "Don't think," she advised in a throaty voice far removed from her usual clear tone. Her hand moved between them, stroking his hard flesh through the worn denim of his jeans. "Just feel, my darling."

Taking his hand, Laurel gave him a seductive, womanly smile as she led him down the hallway to his bedroom. She lay on the vast expanse of water bed, holding her arms out to him, inviting him to join her. Nick needed no further encouragement, gathering her to him for a long, deliriously wonderful kiss. Their clothing was rapidly dispatched, as if burned away by a wildfire, flung to the farthest corners of the room.

The drapes were drawn to the late-afternoon sun, but the darkness in the room seemed to lighten and glow with a fire of its own. As Nick's hands and lips and tongue moved over Laurel's body, he was stunned at the heat of her flesh.

"You're on fire," he murmured, thrilled by her response. "God, how I love it when you burn for me, lovely Laurel."

His hand moved down her body, scorching the flesh of her stomach, trailing sparks down the insides of her thighs and back up again. Laurel gave a little cry of delight.

When his lips moved where his fingers had teased, strange heats burst inside her, little fires that spiraled outward from her innermost core. His tongue became a sensual weapon, probing into the warm satin of her body, and Laurel knew that at any moment she was going to be flung into the reaches of the universe, beyond anything she'd ever experienced, even with Nick. The idea was thrilling, but frightening in its intensity, and she didn't want to go there alone.

"Please, Nick, I need you." Her fingers tangled in his hair as she pulled him up to cover her.

Nick had never known this potential for heat and passion. His body burned, sought, and so did hers. She opened for him and when he plunged into her, it was as if a thousand blazing stars exploded behind his eyes. Laurel responded with a rhythm and ferocity that matched his own, her fingernails raking primitive paths down the moist, rippling muscles of his back.

She wondered how this man could cause every atom in her body to flame; how was it that Nick McGraw could make her toss away every vestige of self-restraint for the sheer, overwhelming feel of his lips against hers, his flesh against her flesh. She wanted to understand—to know what magic this man possessed to make her world continually spin out of control, to make everything and everyone before him commonplace.

But then she was beyond all thought, beyond reason, as their heat exploded into a gigantic white fireball, sending them spinning outward into a world of their own making, a place of blinding lights and vivid colors that swirled about them, enveloping them in the dazzling glow.

Afraid of crushing her, Nick carefully rolled over, still holding her, not yet willing to give up the pleasures of her velvet warmth. The heat gradually faded as they lay together for a long, silent time in the slowly cooling aftermath of passion, her dark hair scented webbing against his chest.

"Laurel?"

"Mmm?" She'd never known such contentment.

"I love you."

She opened her eyes, lifting them to his cautious gaze. "I know," she said simply.

"Any regrets?"

Her smile was beatific. "Regrets? How could I have any regrets? I was just thinking how it would be impossible to be any happier than I am at this moment."

"Are you sure about that?"

"Very sure." She pressed a kiss against his chest.

Nick's hands moved enticingly over the pink-tipped hills of her breasts. "What would you say if I told you I wanted you again?"

Her eyes gleamed a deep ebony as she nodded slowly. "I'd say that I may have been a bit hasty in that assessment."

"Shall we put it to the test?"

Laurel reached up, pulling his head down to her kiss. "Most definitely."

"I'm GOING TO need a doctor if you keep up that wanton behavior," Nick complained a long time later. "I don't think I'll ever move again." He lay beside Laurel, his lashes a golden fringe against his tanned cheeks.

Laurel sighed contentedly. "I know what you mean."

He reached out, his hand unerringly finding her breast. "Happy?"

"I couldn't be happier," she answered honestly.

"How do you really feel about the job?" he asked with a casualness she suspected was feigned. She turned her head, finding him watching her carefully.

Tapping a thoughtful fingernail against her front tooth, Laurel chose her words carefully. "You'd do a wonderful job, Nick. You're terrific with kids."

"I like kids."

She nodded as she considered Nick in that role. He'd be perfect, but would it be enough? "I know," she murmured, lost in thought. "And they all like you."

"Why am I hearing a *but* in that less than enthusiastic response?"

"There's not much fame in youth sports, Nick," she felt obliged to point out. She hadn't come this far to stop being honest with him now.

"I've had enough fame to last me a lifetime, Laurel. Believe me, I'm looking forward to a life of blissful anonymity."

"And fortune. You didn't say what they're paying, but it can't be that generous."

He chuckled. "Now that you're a big shot chief of staff, can't you support a loving husband and a couple of kids?"

Laurel felt herself melting as a light gleamed in his emerald eyes. "A couple?" she whispered.

"Didn't Danny tell you about his master plan? About you and me and a brother or sister?"

"Oh, my God," Laurel groaned. "When did he tell you about that?"

"The first week. It seems like a reasonable enough request to me. In fact, the poor kid's been waiting such a long time, we should probably get started on that little project as soon as possible." He gave her a long, lingering kiss.

"The game," she remembered belatedly. "It's probably still on."

"Forget the game," he murmured, his lips nuzzling at her ear. "I can think of a much better way to spend the day."

"My goodness," she teased, "could this possibly be the same fellow who professed he couldn't separate the man from the football player?"

His teeth bit down lightly on her tender lobe. "It is. But a certain sexy sports doctor once suggested there was more to life than football. Although that idea bordered on heresy, since I didn't have anything better to do, I thought I might as well check it out."

Her fingers played with the thick blond waves curling against the back of his neck. "And what did you find?"

Nick's laugh was deep and filled with satisfaction as he pulled Laurel into his arms. "I found," he said, his kiss pledging a future filled with love, "that there's a lot to be said for indoor sports."

*You're invited to accept 4 books and a surprise gift* **Free!**

# Acceptance Card

**Mail to: Harlequin Reader Service®**

In the U.S.
2504 West Southern Ave.
Tempe, AZ 85282

In Canada
P.O. Box 2800, Postal Station A
5170 Yonge Street
Willowdale, Ontario M2N 6J3

**YES!** Please send me 4 free Harlequin Temptation® novels and my free surprise gift. Then send me 4 brand new novels every month as they come off the presses. Bill me at the low price of $1.99 each ($1.95 in Canada)—a 13% saving off the retail price. There are no shipping, handling or other hidden costs. There is no minimum number of books I must purchase. I can always return a shipment and cancel at any time. Even if I never buy another book from Harlequin, the 4 free novels and the surprise gift are mine to keep forever.

142 BPX-BPGE

Name _____ (PLEASE PRINT)

Address _____ Apt. No. _____

City _____ State/Prov. _____ Zip/Postal Code _____

This offer is limited to one order per household and not valid to present subscribers. Price is subject to change.

ACHT-SUB-1